“Brody, this is bad.”

“Yeah.” Whiteout bad. “I’m thinking I should probably just turn back and we both stay in your little office building tonight?”

“Yes, but be careful. You don’t want to get stuck in a di—”

There was a squeal of tires Brody barely caught over the roar of the wind. He couldn’t see anything, but he felt the impact. Someone had crashed into them. They jerked forward. Brody tried to slam on the brakes, but they got bumped again, so even though he had his foot stomped on the brake, they went forward on the slick road.

Brody kept a death grip on the steering wheel, but the truck was skidding. No, not skidding—*pushed*. Was the car behind them still trying to drive forward? Had the driver lost consciousness with their foot on the gas? Or maybe they were so confused by the storm they didn’t know to stop?

Or...

SMALL TOWN VANISHING

NICOLE HELM

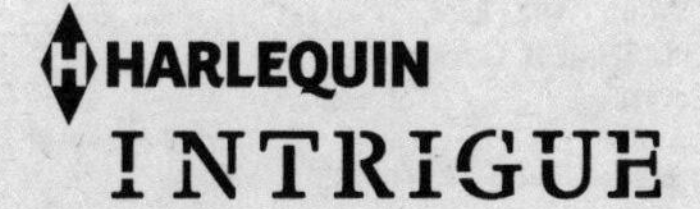

To anyone who preserves the history of extraordinary ordinary people in all the small, weird ways.

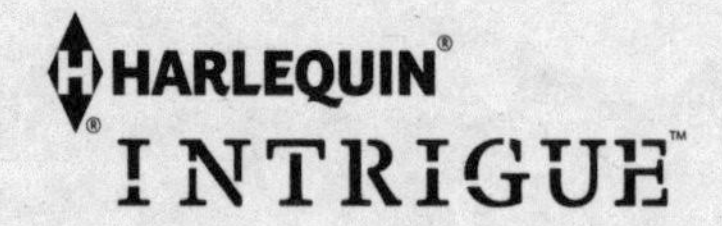

PLEASE RECYCLE
THIS PRODUCT IS RECYCLABLE

Recycling programs for this product may not exist in your area.

ISBN-13: 978-1-335-58225-6

Small Town Vanishing

For questions and comments about the quality of this book, please contact us at CustomerService@Harlequin.com.

Harlequin Enterprises ULC
22 Adelaide St. West, 41st Floor
Toronto, Ontario M5H 4E3, Canada
www.Harlequin.com

Printed in U.S.A.

Nicole Helm grew up with her nose in a book and the dream of one day becoming a writer. Luckily, after a few failed career choices, she gets to follow that dream—writing down-to-earth contemporary romance and romantic suspense. From farmers to cowboys, Midwest to *the* West, Nicole writes stories about people finding themselves and finding love in the process. She lives in Missouri with her husband and two sons, and dreams of someday owning a barn.

Books by Nicole Helm

Harlequin Intrigue

Covert Cowboy Soldiers

The Lost Hart Triplet
Small Town Vanishing

A North Star Novel Series

Summer Stalker
Shot Through the Heart
Mountainside Murder
Cowboy in the Crosshairs
Dodging Bullets in Blue Valley
Undercover Rescue

A Badlands Cops Novel

South Dakota Showdown
Covert Complication
Backcountry Escape
Isolated Threat
Badlands Beware
Close Range Christmas

Visit the Author Profile page at Harlequin.com.

CAST OF CHARACTERS

Kate Phillips—A living history interpreter at a historical fort whose father disappeared ten years ago. Kate has kept searching for him, and when she learns Brody Thompson is good at finding people, she asks him for help on her cold case.

Brody Thompson—Former army ranger, now a rancher, who has to keep his past as a military operative taking down terrorists a secret. But Brody can't resist helping people, and when Kate asks for his expertise, he studies the case and finds the first lead in a decade.

Hazeleigh Hart—Kate's friend and coworker at the historical fort. Lives in a cabin on the Thompson ranch.

Zara Hart—Kate's ex-best friend. Their friendship fell apart when Kate's father disappeared the same day Zara's sister Amberleigh did. Involved with Jake, one of Brody's brothers.

Amberleigh Hart—Disappeared from Wilde at the age of sixteen. Found dead last month on the Thompson ranch.

Jake, Landon, Henry, Dunne and Cal Thompson—Brody's military brothers who live on and work the ranch with him.

Art Phillips—Kate's father who disappeared ten years ago.

Chapter One

Kate Phillips was no stranger to being alone. When your father disappeared the same day as your sixteen-year-old friend, an entire town who had once treated you like a cute eccentric could decide you were pariah by association.

Her mother hadn't helped. Marjorie Phillips had blamed *everyone* in the town of Wilde, Wyoming, for the disappearance of her husband—in dramatic, screaming theatrics for a decade now.

Which, yet again, made Kate guilty by association. Or at least, someone to avoid.

Kate could have withstood that, she was certain, if she hadn't lost her best friends in the process. The problem was that Kate's only friends growing up had been the Hart triplets. Different though they were, the four of them had been an inseparable group. Constantly in each other's pockets.

Then Amberleigh had disappeared the same day as Dad, and Hazeleigh and Zara had treated her differently ever since. Hazeleigh had slowly come around. Hard not to when both Kate and Hazeleigh worked at the Fort Dry Historic Site, Wilde's historical landmark. Hazeleigh doing research for the supervisor at the fort, Mr. Field, and Kate as a living history interpreter and tour guide.

But Zara had *not* come around. Pointedly so.

So, Kate's life had come down to two things: her angry mother and her job. At least Kate loved the job. She knew Wildeans tended to pity her when they weren't suspicious of her, but this job was the one thing that felt…normal in a life that had changed a decade ago.

Normal to be alone, doing some work dressing mannequins, the day after Christmas. In a drafty old historical building that likely wouldn't have visitors until the summer months.

Still, she liked to change out the displays. Focus on the past, rather than her present.

Mr. Field was in his office, so she wasn't *totally* alone. He might shut himself up in there and not say two words to her, but that was still more companionship than she had in her small attic room with Mom. Mostly, despite living in the same sprawling house, their paths rarely crossed. Mom's choice. Insistence, really.

It was for the best. Kate had been happier since they'd nonverbally agreed to keep their distance—as long as Kate did all the errands and everything that was expected of her. But happier didn't negate the loneliness. She'd get some kind of animal if she weren't allergic, but everything hypoallergenic gave her the creeps.

Kate sighed. She could do lonely. She was *good* at lonely. But lonely at Christmas—a holiday Mom hadn't celebrated in ten years—was a different kind, a deeper kind of lonesome, and she couldn't wait for the calendar to switch over to the new year. Put the ten-year anniversary behind her.

She heard the door squeak open and finished tying the apron on the mannequin, telling herself not to run to see who the visitor was like a desperately sad inmate.

"Did you hear?" came Hazeleigh's voice, a few seconds before she appeared—all pastel layers and wild curly brown hair. "They found Eli Mayfield."

"Really?" The missing boy had disappeared from Wilde some time the night of Christmas Eve, at least that's what Kate had read in the paper. According to the sporadically updated town Facebook page, the police had begun to get desperate last night due to the frigid temperatures and the boy's young age, and Kate had been reminded of all the awful ways a disappearance could strangle just about everyone in town.

"Safe, and sound, and not a moment too soon," Hazeleigh continued, unwinding a fluffy pink scarf she no doubt had knitted herself. "The doctors are saying he could have been dead from exposure if he'd been out there another few hours."

"Thank goodness." Kate meant it, though she wasn't sure she sounded as relieved as she should have. A seven-year-old didn't deserve to just disappear, or worse. But Kate couldn't help but think of her own father. Dead? Alive? Gone on purpose? Gone against his will?

It had been ten years, and she knew she should move

on. Give up. Wasn't that what her mother always told her? But Kate never could bring herself to.

And finding out last week that it was very possible Amberleigh's same-day disappearance had very little to do with her father brought up new questions.

"How…how was he found?" Kate asked, trying to find the right way to handle this. She was *relieved* the young boy had been found. Not jealous someone had been found when her father hadn't.

"It was Jake's brother Brody who found him," Hazeleigh said. The six Thompson brothers had bought the Hart Ranch and had been working it for the past almost two months. Kate didn't know all of them by name, but she knew Jake as he'd been instrumental in helping get Hazeleigh cleared of the murder charge that had been leveled against her.

December had been a busy month in Wilde.

"Jake was telling Zara that if something is lost, Brody's always the one to find it. I'm not sure how Brody managed, but apparently he was out all last night and found the boy. I'm so glad he did. Apparently poor Eli just got turned around trying to prove to his friend he could climb Mount Hopkins higher than anyone."

Kate nodded. "I suppose it's a relief to everyone he just wandered off." *Wasn't stolen. Wasn't like when Art Phillips went off with a* teenager.

"I'm going to go tell Mr. Field."

Kate nodded as Hazeleigh wafted over to Mr. Field's office. Kate looked at the mannequin she'd been dressing, but for once she wasn't thinking about the frontier. She was thinking about her *own* past.

Where something had been lost.

Jake was telling Zara that if something is lost, Brody's always the one to find it.

Well, maybe the mysterious Brody Thompson was someone she should get to know.

"IT HAD TO be done." Brody looked at Cal, scowling in the driver's seat. After spending a few hours with the police and a very grateful Mayfield family, Brody wanted quiet, something hot to eat and maybe a beer. But as many questions as the police might have asked him, he knew it was only a precursor to this.

Getting chewed out by his *brother.* "We're talking about a missing kid here."

"I know what we're talking about," Cal returned, his grip on the truck's steering wheel tight enough to make his knuckles white. "I just don't know how you all seem to expect me to be able to keep us here if you and Jake are constantly getting your name in the papers."

Because somehow Wilde, Wyoming, still depended on the local paper for its news. It was like stepping back in time, this new life Brody found himself in.

He was surprised to find he didn't hate it, and much like their *brother* Jake, Brody wanted to stay.

"You were part of the search, Cal," Brody reminded the man who'd once been his commanding officer, but these days had to pretend to be nothing more than his ranching brother.

Cal didn't do *blending in* as well as he thought he did. He also wasn't as hard as he fancied himself. Though he'd tried to keep it on the down low, Brody knew that

Cal had stood up to the boss when Jake had found himself in some trouble.

Brody wasn't comfortable thinking about how much trouble Jake had gotten himself in, or how jumping in front of a bullet meant for Cal had almost cost him his life. Jake was alive, and the boss was off their backs.

Perhaps not now that Brody had gotten a little local notoriety—even if Wilde local meant about fifty people.

The issue was that Brody would have his name in the paper so closely after Jake's. No time for the town to get bored of the Thompson brothers. Which meant attention and perhaps poking into their pasts. Which was a no go.

Because the men of Team Breaker—who didn't exist anymore—were supposed to move to Wilde and disappear. Not make a name for themselves.

But it was a *kid.* "The boss is going to have to accept that anywhere we live, we're part of the community. It's ecosystems, plain and simple."

Cal grumbled some intelligible words but didn't otherwise mount an argument.

Who could argue against ecosystems?

Cal turned off on the gravel road that would take them to the ranch. Brody had been born and bred in the Chicago suburbs. He might have had more awareness of the existence of agriculture than his friends from New York City, but that didn't mean squat in the face of the reality of a ranch.

But he'd learned. He'd tackled the task of learning how to be a rancher like he'd taken to the task of becoming an army ranger. Ordinary didn't suffice for Brody

Calhoun—Thompson these days. No, his parents had been so below ordinary and capable that Brody did everything in his power to stay as far above the pack as he could.

He was always the first to volunteer for whatever task their ranch hand, Zara Hart, had to teach them. It was winter, so the learning curve wasn't too steep. Come spring, they better know what they were doing.

Come hell or high water, Brody would know what he was doing. And exceptionally well.

They drove under the archway that still read Hart Ranch, though the Harts didn't own it anymore. Zara Hart had stayed on as ranch hand, and she and her sister Hazeleigh still lived in a cabin on ranch property, but the ranch was now the property of Team Breaker.

Known in Wilde as the Thompson brothers.

Cal drove the winding lane toward the house. Brody appreciated the Wyoming views. They were pretty, as grand and picturesque as everything he'd been told about the Wild West as a kid, but it was the house that did something to him.

Brody had grown up in apartments, spent months on the street when his dad had gone through a "rough patch" and Mom had disappeared. The big rambling house situated in the rolling hills, bracketed by far off mountains was…beyond a dream. Brody's dreams had been excellence in the military.

This was something else, and he still wasn't comfortable with the way that something else swelled inside him like a storm. A wild howling thing that would die if it ever got taken away.

Dramatic.

"Who the hell is that?" Cal grumbled as he pulled up to the house. A woman paced the big wraparound porch, something clasped in her hands.

Brody frowned. Something about her was familiar but he couldn't put his finger on it, so he and Cal got out of the truck at the same time and surveyed the woman from afar.

She stopped pacing, staring right back at them, but she neither approached nor offered a greeting until they walked up to the porch.

She stood on the top stair like she belonged there and was greeting strangers to her house. But when they both came to stop at the bottom of the stairs, she attempted a smile. It frayed around the edges.

"Hi."

Brody and Cal exchanged glances.

"I'm… K-kate. Kate Phillips? I work with Hazeleigh. Uh, the last time we met I was dressed up like a pioneer."

Brody knew laughing wasn't the polite thing to do, but it was a hard-won thing. She *had* been dressed like a pioneer at that crazy little fort where Hazeleigh worked. When Jake had begged him to go along with Zara and Hazeleigh to some living history Christmas thing, Brody had done it simply because Jake had been shot, and that and Christmas had softened Brody enough to agree.

This woman *had* been there, dressed up in pioneer clothes, lecturing the small group on Christmas in Wilde, Wyoming, something like centuries ago. He remembered finding himself a little interested against his will. Brody couldn't say he hated the way she'd been dressed either. There was something…endlessly interesting about all those layers and what they might be hiding underneath.

But Kate Phillips looked just as prim and pretty in jeans and a big puffer jacket standing on his porch.

Funny how it could feel like *his* porch.

"I brought cookies," she blurted out, shoving a plastic bag at him.

"For Jake?" Cal asked, clearly confused.

"Not exactly." She sucked in a deep breath, and she didn't look at Cal. She stared right at him, brown eyes deep and a little heartbreakingly desperate. "I have someone I need help finding."

Brody didn't wince, he'd been in the military too long to outwardly react. Besides, Cal reacted enough for the both of them.

"I'm sorry, that won't be possible."

Kate's entire expression fell, like a building taken out by an inside explosion. But she managed to stop the crumple right before it destroyed everything. She straightened her shoulders and looked at Cal coolly. "I wasn't asking you."

Cal was clearly taken aback by how quickly she'd changed from nervous stutter to cold put-down. It made Brody smile.

"Why don't you go on inside, Cal? I'll handle this."

"Yeah, I just bet you will." He glared at Kate. "Look, miss, you might be friends with Hazeleigh, but this isn't some—"

"Cal, it's only *neighborly* to hear her out. You go on inside. Think ecosystems."

Cal turned his glare on him, shook his head, but didn't say another word before stalking inside, the door slamming behind him.

Kate frowned after him. "He's charming."

Brody didn't say what he wanted—that she should see him supervising a deadly mission in the Middle East—because here he wasn't Brody Calhoun, army ranger, and Cal wasn't Cal Young, lead on a secret mission to take down a terrorist target.

They were just ranchers. From here on out.

So he smiled at Kate and went for sarcasm instead. "Devastatingly so." Brody studied the cookies in the bag she'd shoved at him. He'd been up all night looking for the Mayfield boy and he'd barely eaten. He pulled one from the bag. "Is someone missing?" Brody asked.

"In a manner of speaking. Hazeleigh said Zara said Jake said—"

"Maybe you shouldn't take everything you hear fourth-hand so seriously."

"Technically it was only third-hand."

He held up his fingers and put them down with every point. "Jake. Zara. Hazeleigh. You."

She mimicked his position. "Jake told Zara." She put down one finger. "Zara told Hazeleigh." Another finger. "Hazeleigh to me. That's three."

Brody laughed. He knew humoring this woman wasn't going to make his life any easier, but he couldn't help it. Someone needed help—and it had been seared into his bones to help where he could.

He was well aware of all the places he couldn't help.

He popped the cookie into his mouth. Good. No, not just good. Exceptional. "You can bake, Kate Phillips. Are these supposed to be a bribe?"

"Yes," she said solemnly. "Did they work?"

"We'll see. Why don't you come inside, and we'll talk it over where it's warm?"

She pulled the coat she wore tighter around her. "I'm fine out here."

"Cal won't bite. Promise."

"No, but Zara will."

"Uh, well…" Brody didn't know what to say to that. Zara might live in the cabin on the property, but ever since Jake had come home yesterday, Zara had been a constant presence in the house, repeatedly telling the *likes of them* that men were terrible at caring for the wounded.

No one had dared argue with her.

It was a strange phenomenon Brody hadn't fully worked out, considering the six of them had stood up to a lot worse than a mouthy ranch hand.

But Jake was in love with Zara, whatever that meant, and Jake was hurt, and…

Bottom line was Brody had gotten himself into enough hot water. Time to slow things down. "I'd like to help, but…"

"But you won't. Because of Zara."

"Listen—"

"No, I get it. Believe me," she said, pushing past him, "I get it."

It was the glimmer of tears in her eyes that just about

killed him. Brody could withstand a lot of things. But he was a sucker for tears, even ones that didn't fall.

"You haven't even told me who's missing," he called after her.

She stopped at the little sedan that seemed so out of place in this harsh Wyoming winter. "My father disappeared ten years ago," she shot at him. "With Zara's sister, at least that was the rumor. That…speculation has been my life for ten years. Now we know Amberleigh Hart is dead, and she wasn't with my father. I want to find him, but if Queen Zara is in charge here, then—"

Brody heard the screen door squeak behind him, and he knew without looking Zara would be standing there. Just by the shocked, guilty, then back to furious expressions that stormed over Kate's pretty face.

"What am I queen of?"

Kate stood there for a moment, somehow looking both furious and deeply wounded at the same time before she got into her car and slammed the door. She didn't *peel* away, but she certainly drove off in a hurry.

"What was that about?" Brody asked, turning to face Zara.

Zara shrugged, her eyes on the retreating car. "Let me guess. She wants you to find her father."

"Yeah."

"You should."

"Huh?"

Zara blew out a breath. "Look, I don't know if I really believe her dad didn't have *anything* to do with Amberleigh's disappearance, but he didn't kill Amberleigh."

Zara frowned at where Kate had disappeared. "Trying to find closure sucks, but Kate deserves some."

"I don't think I'm the one to give it to her."

Zara turned her dark gaze on him. "You find things, Brody." She smiled faintly. "That's your expertise, isn't it?"

He supposed it was, and the need to live up to it had him taking the address Zara gave him and following Kate home.

Chapter Two

It had been a long time since Kate had felt fully paranoid. That first year after everything had imploded she'd found herself looking around every corner, over her shoulder, constantly holding her breath and waiting for her father to step out of the shadows.

Her schoolwork had suffered, her *life* had suffered, but she'd made it through somehow. Mostly by focusing on taking care of her mother and spending whatever free time she had finding her father.

Eventually, as her job at the fort had begun to fulfill her, she'd let some of the search obsession fade away. She had a job and Mom still needed looking after. She'd tried to step away from the one giant mystery of her life.

But ever since Amberleigh's body had been found on the Hart Ranch a few weeks ago, Kate had felt like she had at sixteen.

Edgy. Paranoid. Desperate. She'd started poring over her old research. Trying to reconstruct what she knew. Trying to tell herself new leads might help her to…

She went into the market and picked up a few things Mom needed. Things *were* different, ever since the news of Amberleigh's death had spread. The stares were back. The whispers. And because Mom tended to yell, accuse and melt down when those things happened, everyone kept their distance.

No one asked how she was. No one...

She swallowed. She couldn't let the things that had happened this month change all the personal progress she'd made. She didn't *need* anyone in town to care about her. She had her job and her responsibilities. She had coworkers she could ask a favor of as long as Mr. Field wasn't busy and Hazeleigh didn't have to think too hard about why they'd grown apart in the first place.

Everything was *fine*. Who cared if people watched her get into her car? Who cared if Mom was likely to yell at her for being late when she got home? Who *cared?*

She had built walls around the hard things and given herself some good things and *that* was what she cared about. She drove down Main Street and then up the curving drive to the house that stood on the top of a hill, above the town like the Phillips were better than everyone.

The house, the grounds, none of it had been well taken care of since Dad left. They should have sold it before it had gotten this dilapidated, but Mom refused, and Kate only had so much access to money to accomplish repairs.

But the house stood, and it was something of a legacy. Wasn't that more than Zara and Hazeleigh had? Maybe they got to stay on the Hart Ranch, but it wasn't *theirs* anymore.

Kate just wished she could feel any kind of pride in her legacy.

She had to get these downer thoughts under control before she went inside though. Kate needed to build back the wall the past few weeks had crumbled.

She got out of her car, grabbing the overly-full grocery bag. It was too heavy a weight and she should probably switch it to one of the canvas bags she had in the back, but—

The bottom gave out, the cans hitting the driveway with a *clank, clank, clank*. Kate managed to catch a few before they fell, but a few went rolling down the driveway, gathering speed. Kate lurched to grab as many cans as she could and upend them so they didn't roll away. But one slipped through her grasp, picking up speed as it went, until it landed with a thud against the bottom of a boot.

A cowboy boot. She looked up, surprised to see Brody Thompson standing there. She hadn't seen his truck, hadn't heard him approach. She supposed because the truck was at the bottom of the drive. He'd walked up and…

"What are you doing here?"

He bent down and picked up the can from under his foot, then crossed to her and held it out. She took it, but she didn't know quite what to do with it.

His eyes tracked around the array of cans of soup on her driveway. Then he looked straight at her, something like…she wanted to call it pity, but it didn't *feel* like any pity she'd ever gotten, and boy, she'd gotten her share.

"I'll help you, if I can," he said quietly. Seriously.

She studied him for the longest time, trying to understand his change of heart. Trying to understand... But then it dawned on her. She was so pitiful even Zara—who *hated* her for what her father had supposedly done with Amberleigh—had given Brody the okay to help.

She wished she were too proud to take it, but she wasn't. Ten years in, she was still as desperate for answers as she'd always been. If she got answers—even if they were the bad kind—she could close that chapter of her life. Maybe leave Wilde. Maybe...

If she could find the answers, her life could finally change.

She glanced back at the house. Mom would not be okay with any of this. They couldn't have this conversation here. Just because Zaza might have given Brody the okay did not mean Kate had to hang out at the Hart Ranch like she was a little girl again.

"Maybe we could talk about this at the fort? Tomorrow morning?"

He frowned a little, looked at the big, rambling but rundown house behind her. "Someone you're hiding from?"

How to explain? There was no easy answer.

"If it's a husband, or boyfriend, or whatever, I'd make sure to let him know—"

"A...boyfriend," she repeated. The word felt foreign. Like it belonged to a different universe. Certainly not one she was a part of.

Brody flashed her a grin, "If I lived with a pretty woman, I wouldn't want her hanging out with a strange man at some isolated fort."

Pretty…woman. She was truly and utterly speechless. *Pretty woman* said with that hint of some kind of regional accent she couldn't place. And that grin. Which she might have characterized as flirtatious if it were aimed at anyone else.

"I live with my mother."

He nodded, as if that was also an acceptable answer. "Yeah, I'm not popular with moms."

"She doesn't… She wouldn't like…" Kate blew out a breath. If she expected help, she needed to get a hold of herself. "I'd prefer to discuss all this away from her. It upsets her, understandably. Besides, I keep all my research in my office at the fort."

"Research?"

"I've been searching for my father for a decade. I have plenty of research."

Brody frowned at that. "It's been a long time. You've done a lot of work. You have to know that even with my help, the chances of finding him are slim."

"I know. Believe me, plenty of people haven't been able to. I'm not expecting miracles. I just can't seem to…" She struggled to find the words. *Let go? Get over it? Move on?* "I just have to use whatever I can to try and solve this." And she had to focus on practicalities not the complex tangle of emotions battering her insides. "I can't really pay you, so if that's a deal-breaker—"

He gave the house a look, totally inscrutable. "I don't need payment. Except maybe in cookies. We'll just consider it a favor for a friend."

"I'm not your friend."

"Zara is...something like a friend, but mostly I mean Jake. He's all gaga over Zara, so..." Brody shrugged.

She wished she knew what that kind of loyal friendship was like, but that wasn't the point. "Tomorrow morning? Is eight all right?"

"Sure." He looked at the cans littered around them. "You need some help?"

Help. She wanted to laugh. When was the last time anyone had offered something like help? "No, I've got it."

BRODY DIDN'T TELL anyone what he was doing. He figured Zara would mention it to Jake, but with Jake relegated mostly to bed, and Zara hovering over him like a private nurse, Brody wasn't too worried about what Jake knew.

When Cal asked about that Kate woman, Brody changed the subject.

Best to see what was what first. Finding lost things people didn't want found *was* his expertise after all, not anybody else's. Back when Team Breaker had received their assignment, Brody had been the one to find the terrorist cell's home base.

Too bad some of their intel had been faulty.

He pushed that thought away and parked his truck in the lot of Fort Dry Historic Site. Snow was piled up around all three buildings that made up the fort, but the walks were ruthlessly cleared. Salt put down to keep the ice at bay. The site was surrounded on all sides by flat snow-covered land, the mountains far off in the distance.

A door opened and Kate stood there, waving him over. She was dressed in jeans and a sweatshirt when he'd kind of expected her to be in her historical getup.

The odd feeling spiraling through him was disappointment. He rather enjoyed her all dressed up, looking like some ghost from the past. "Thought you'd be in your costume."

"We don't officially open until ten," she said primly, having to look up at him as he approached. She wasn't short exactly, but he was tall and so he towered over her a little bit.

She didn't seem all that concerned about his size and being alone together, whereas Hazeleigh was *just* getting used to not jumping a foot when he or his brothers approached. Kate didn't seem at all *afraid* of him. Her nerves all seemed to stem from the topic at hand.

She led him into the small building that seemed more offices and storage than historical facility. Her office was small, and he hesitated following her inside, considering they'd be basically on top of each other.

And he was a little too intrigued by the prospect.

He hung by the door, but she marched in and pulled a crate from under her desk. Then she moved to a filing cabinet and pulled out an entire arm full of folders. She put them on top of the crate. "This is just what I've got in print. I keep some things on my computer too."

He looked at the sheer volume of information. She had more on her father's disappearance than he'd had on the leader of the terrorist organization Team Breaker had been after.

"Kate..."

"I know, you think because I did all this you won't be able to find him."

"It's not that exactly." He *excelled* at finding people, even when the circumstances said no one would find them. This was more about all the work and hours she'd put into this disappearance. All the hope she clearly had that her father could be found, and probably with a happy-ending kind of result.

In Brody's mind, happy endings didn't come after all *this*. "Maybe he doesn't want to be found."

"And maybe he's dead," she said flatly, putting to words what he'd really wanted to say. "I know the possibilities. I know that the chances of me finding something that makes me feel better is slim to none. I don't need happy endings, Brody. I just need answers. Closure."

He nodded. "All right. I'll see what I can do. Do you mind if I take this back to the house?"

She studied the information and chewed on her bottom lip, a slightly distracting movement because she had a very *interesting* mouth.

Yeah, it had been a while since he'd been in the consistent, solitary company of a woman. And Kate was the…fragile kind. Well, fragile wasn't the right word. She'd held up under losing her father and trying to find him. She was vulnerable maybe, and a little naive. Not his type.

His body wasn't getting the memo.

"I'd rather keep everything here. It's safer here. We could just look through stuff and I could explain anything to you. I know you have a ranch to run. I don't expect you to just… I don't know."

She sighed and lowered herself into a rickety-looking chair. "I didn't really think this through. Hazeleigh said Zara said Jake said…" She trailed off, smiled up at him a little. "Yes, I know, third-hand and all, but when she said you knew how to find things… Maybe if I'd heard that a month ago, it wouldn't have mattered, but with Amberleigh's body being found…"

She shook her head. "She was my friend too, you know. Maybe not my sister, but my friend."

"You were close with all of them." It didn't need to be a question. The palpable *emotion* was evidence enough.

"Yes. But it was Zara and I… We were best friends." Kate shrugged as if shrugging away that emotion, but it lingered. In her eyes. "I was close with the triplets. We grew up together. My father was a teacher at the high school. Very well respected. My parents were sort of a golden couple. Mom from a well-to-do family, my father from a wrong-side-of-the-tracks family who'd pulled himself up by his bootstraps to get an education, then come back and serve the community." She shook her head. "Neither here nor there, I guess."

"It all helps when you're trying to find someone. You never know what might help."

She blew out a breath. "One day Dad didn't show up to work. And Amberleigh didn't show up to school. There was never any evidence they disappeared together, but they both disappeared the same day and, well… I suppose it's natural what people came to believe."

"That they had an affair?"

Kate shrugged again, but it was jerkier.

"Was there any evidence of an affair?"

"Nothing concrete. But enough that looking back over it, people wondered. Amberleigh liked to hang out at my house, even though we had more freedom at the Hart Ranch. She took violin lessons with me and my father, and Dad gave her private lessons for free—presumably because her father wouldn't have paid for them, but people put…other reasons behind it."

Yikes. Brody wasn't sure what to say to that.

"My mother denied it vehemently, and so did I. Amberleigh was… She liked to shock people. Men especially. She'd said a few things that I'd never thought twice about, but the police really liked that angle. Which meant all that was left was for the town to shun the entire family."

"Guilt by association?"

"Pretty much."

Brody didn't know how to outwardly react given the sensitive situation. He changed the subject instead. "But Zara didn't blame your father. She blamed you?"

"It isn't that simple. And like I said, neither here nor there." She picked up a folder. "These were the initial missing persons reports for my father and Amberleigh."

Brody took the outstretched papers and skimmed over them. Nothing connecting the two beyond circumstantial sorts of things. Nothing left behind—no note, no hints. Just one day they were there, and the next they weren't.

He looked up from the papers to see her standing there, hands clasped so hard her knuckles were white.

A brittle expression on her face that suggested she was working very hard to hold herself together—and was definitely old hat at it.

He couldn't quite work Kate Phillips out. She didn't fit into any neat box. At turns awkward, nervous, bitter, determined.

"You've certainly had a rough go of it, haven't you?"

She startled, looking arrested, big dark eyes meeting his. "Me?"

"Well, sure, you were the one caught in the middle."

Chapter Three

Kate had to fight back the emotion that threatened to swallow her whole. She didn't know Brody Thompson, and he didn't know her. She supposed that was why he could look at this with such a lack of bias.

Caught in the middle?

She shook her head. "Not that simple."

"Seems simple to me. Your dad and your friend disappeared. I'm assuming a good half the town blamed your father and you by default. When bad things happen in a small community, everyone has something to say about it and the people involved."

"Are you well versed in small towns?" she asked, because it hit too hard, too close to the bone when all that scar tissue she'd built up was supposed to keep her safe.

He smiled enigmatically, but there was something very…deep behind that smile. Not humorous, at least to him. "Something like that." He hefted the boxes easily. "You've got somewhere with a little more surface area for us to work?"

"There's a conference room in the back."

He nodded, then jerked his chin as a sign for her to

lead the way. He carried *all* of it like it were nothing. Which gave Kate a little flutter low in her stomach.

For a moment Kate had the strangest sensation she'd stepped into a dream world. This couldn't be real. Help from a very nice-looking man. Who was friendly and polite and was supposed to know how to find people.

Ten years, no one had helped. No one had been *polite.*

She blinked when he raised an eyebrow at her. *Right.* She exited her office, skirting him with as much room as she could—a little afraid if she got too close, looked too hard, he'd disappear in a puff of smoke like the mirage he must be.

She led him to the conference room and turned on the lights. It was frigid. "I can go grab the space heater from my office."

He waved her off. "I'm fine." He dropped the crate on the long table and studied them, even though he couldn't know what was in them. But it was like he was doing some kind of mathematical calculation.

"Day of information here." He pointed to a spot on the table. "Police reports and the like from then on out." He moved a little ways down. "Anything leading up to the disappearance." And so on until he expected her to make five piles of the information.

"That's not how I've been organizing things."

He shrugged. "It's how I need to organize things." Then he just stood there…waiting for her to get to work. She couldn't say she *liked* being ordered around, but she was used to it, wasn't she? Reorganizing her life, reshaping *herself* to suit the needs of everyone around her. Her mother, the town.

And you survived by doing all that. So she moved forward and began to organize in the way he'd instructed her. But Brody didn't sit idly by. He helped, creating a human chain. She told him what something was, he put it in the appropriate spot.

They'd gotten through almost all of it when Kate glanced up at the wall clock. "I have to go get ready for my shift."

He waved her off. "Yeah, go ahead."

"You want to…stay?"

"I just got started. I'll let you know before I go."

"All this has to be put up and away. I don't think we have any groups who've rented the room, but—"

He waved her away again. "I'll handle it."

I'll handle it. Had anyone said that to her since that fateful day ten years ago? Because it seemed like she had been stepping up to handle *everything* since Dad disappeared.

But Brody Thompson was going to *handle it*, and Kate didn't have the first clue what to do about that.

ONCE BRODY GOT everything set up the way he needed, he started going through all Kate's files. She'd kept meticulous records—not just police reports and credit card statements, but notes on people she'd talked to or people who'd talked to *her*.

It was impressive, really. Obsessive, possibly, but Brody wasn't a stranger to being obsessive himself. And as it made his task easier, he was mostly grateful for it.

He got lost in it all, building a picture in his mind of what that day looked like. He made his own notes, began compiling his own theories, and yes, came to some conclusions.

Like, there would have to be some pretty amazing explanation for why these two people disappeared on the same day if it wasn't together.

A crick began to form in his neck, reminding him he wasn't as young as he used to be. When he looked up to stretch out his neck, he found her standing there in the doorway. She was dressed in her getup—all layers of fabric, big skirts, even a bonnet.

His heart thumped once, *hard* against his chest. Some out-of-body premonition before everything went back to normal.

He'd felt that thing a time or two—usually before some *really* bad things went down. But he wasn't in the military any longer. He was in a tiny town in the-middle-of-nowhere Wyoming under an assumed name.

Helping a woman dressed like she belonged in a covered wagon find her father who—by all accounts—had left of his own accord.

But *why*.

"I have to close up the building." She was frowning at him, as if she didn't understand what was going on in front of her even though she knew exactly what he'd been doing. She'd *asked* him to do it. "You've been at this all day. I..."

Brody looked down at his watch. The break with his concentration made him realize he was *starving*.

"Did you even eat anything?"

Brody ran his hand through his hair. He'd been deep in it and it was taking a few seconds for him to emerge from the facts of the case to refocus his brain on the present. "Ah, no. Got kind of lost in the research."

"Well, I certainly know that feeling, but you should eat." She studied the table, but didn't say anything else. She wasn't going to ask if he'd found anything. Somehow that made him feel sympathetic, when it wouldn't do either of them any good for him to try to make her feel better.

"I think I've got a line to tug."

"A line… Really? That quickly?"

He shrugged, not wanting to get her hopes up, though he could practically see the way she was trying to hold herself back from hope. A woman who'd been burned a few too many times.

Which meant he was playing with fire. Something he'd promised himself not to do anymore, but… Old habits died hard. "Did you ever really look at the financials, Kate?"

"Of course. I pored over his credit card records. His bank statements. But nothing out of the ordinary."

He wished he could agree. "Unfortunately, there are a few charges on that credit card that don't add up."

"That's impossible."

Brody didn't say anything. She didn't want to believe him, not his problem. So, he just waited.

She closed her eyes and sighed, pushing her fingers against her temples. "Not impossible, of course. I just… I spent so much time on them."

"There were multiple charges to a place called Stanley Music."

"My father was a music teacher. Charges to anything music related make sense."

"But they don't. There's a pattern to the payments he made, and to the private lessons Amberleigh took."

"It could have been sheet music. Supplies. Private lessons would necessitate some personal cost, even if he wasn't charging her for the lessons. We could afford it."

"Sure. But I looked up Stanley Music. I couldn't find one. Not in Wyoming. Not in the entire United States that fit the information on the statement."

"Maybe they went out of business."

As if Brody didn't look that up too, but he could see she needed her suggestion to be a possibility so he just shrugged. "Maybe."

"But you don't think so. You think it means something."

"I think it's a lead to tug. That's all."

She let out a slow breath. Then tried a very sad attempt at a smile. "All right, then we'll tug on it. But first, you must be starving. I owe you a meal."

"You said you couldn't pay me."

"I can't. But I can feed you."

Chapter Four

There was a small kitchen in the back of the main fort building. Mr. Field looked to be gone for the day, so Kate didn't have to worry about explaining Brody to him.

"You just make yourself comfortable. I'll change, then I can whip something up in about ten minutes."

"You don't have to do this."

"I'd feel a lot better if I did. And it's nothing. I just keep a few things here on the off chance I get caught in the snow."

"With that tiny car, I'm surprised you don't have to stay here all the time."

"A truck would be more convenient." And expensive. "But I don't mind staying out here when I have to. It's like…" She trailed off, feeling heat creep up her cheeks. Brody was nice and all, but that didn't mean she needed to confess every history nerd aspect of her lonely life. "Well, it's just fine. Be right back."

She left him there, went and changed quickly into her modern clothes, then returned to him on his phone.

He didn't look up, so she got out a skillet, precooked

chicken breast slices and some frozen vegetables to put together in a quick little stir-fry.

Deep down, she liked to get snowed in here. It meant she didn't have to go home to the ghosts of her father, the anger of her mother coating every inch of the house even though they kept their distance. Here she could pretend she'd chosen a life of adventure and possibility out on the prairie and being all alone was simply a necessary component of that westward dream.

"What about that Mr. Field or Hazeleigh? They never stick around to drive you home in bad weather?"

"Oh, Mr. Field doesn't live far off. In the winter he usually just snowmobiles over. Or stays home if he's a mind to. Hazeleigh doesn't drive much, and the truck is Zara's. Besides, she's just Mr. Field's research assistant, so she's more beholden to him than the fort." She shrugged. "I don't mind. Really."

"I thought rural folks were supposed to be all neighborly and helpful."

"They are." She moved the food around in the pan. "I'm…complicated."

"I don't think you're the complicated one, Kate."

"No, but if you ever meet my mother, you'll know why people would rather keep out of it."

Brody frowned at her as she scooped the food from pan to plate. She didn't meet his gaze, but she could feel it all the same. He was trying to size her up. Make sense of her.

Good luck, buddy.

"My mother was no prize, so I understand that I suppose," he muttered, watching her with such intense study that Kate kept her gaze on the plate as she slid it in front of him. Before she could retreat, maybe make excuses about needing to clean up and leave him to eat, he reached for her wrist.

That should probably be alarming rather than a little thrilling. *You really have absolutely no life.*

"You're going to sit down and eat some of this yourself. Go on and get yourself a plate."

"I'm not really—"

He raised an eyebrow at her.

"You're very used to telling people what to do, aren't you?"

"*Very,*" he said, but with a smile so it felt…friendly. Like they were sharing a moment rather than she was getting bossed around. He let go of her wrist, and because she was nothing if not a biddable soldier, she got herself a plate and let Brody serve up some of the food she'd made on it.

He gestured to the seat across from him at the tiny table, and she took it. He was doing her a favor after all. Without pay. Why not do as she was told?

Besides, she *was* hungry. She took a bite and then looked up at him. The Thompson brothers were Wilde mysteries. No one had a clear idea where they'd come from, what brought them here or why they all looked and sounded so different.

"How'd you wind up in Wyoming?" Kate asked casually. She was rather used to trying to get to the bottom of mysteries.

Brody stared hard at his plate before flashing a smile.

"Oh, this and that. Cal's sort of the de facto leader. I go where he goes."

"You talk differently than he does."

"Do I?" He shrugged. "We weren't raised together. We're a motley crew of brothers—half, step and adopted. Maybe that's why we stick together now."

"That's…sweet."

His eyebrows shot up for a second and then he relaxed into another smile. "Not something we're accused of being all that often."

She thought of the six brothers. They were all big and intimidating looking, no matter how some of them smiled and clearly tried to lend a friendly air to their interactions in town. There was something…different about them, and it wasn't just that they weren't from around here.

"Well, if you keep cooking for me like this, I might just have to marry you."

She tried to laugh, but it came out strained to her own ears. She did not know what to do with anyone making *marrying* jokes, let alone a man that looked like Brody Thompson. He was just so…tall. And muscular. Most of the men she knew were more a rangy sort. Or had that older rancher paunch that seemed to settle over them all eventually. But Brady was *built.* Like an actor in one of those superhero movies. Then there were his eyes, which were an intriguing maze of hazel.

None of which is very applicable to your life, Kate. Get it together.

They finished eating, and Kate quickly cleaned up. She felt Brody's eyes on her the whole time, and while she might have indulged in one quick fantasy that he was looking at her because he liked what he saw, she knew better.

He was trying to figure her out. She was a puzzle for him to solve. That and pity were the only reasons he was helping her.

But, without being asked, he stepped in to help dry the dishes.

"I should get back to the ranch, but I'll look into this Stanley Music mystery more. Maybe there's an innocent explanation."

And maybe there's not. "If there's any kind of answer there, I want it. Good or bad. I can handle it."

He looked down at her, and she felt a careful study. Like he was determining for himself if she could.

After a moment or two, he nodded. It was as much agreement as she could expect, she supposed.

She led him back through the building again and out the front door. They stepped out into the frigid dark. Kate locked the door, and when she turned, she noticed big fat snowflakes fell from the sky. The walk was already covered by the new snowfall. His truck windshield was dusted as well.

"Why don't you let me drive you home?" Brody said.

"You don't have to worry about that."

"No trouble. Easy in my truck."

"I'll stay here tonight. No worries." She motioned to the smaller building. "I've still got some cleanup to do."

"I—"

"Thank you for all your help today." She stuck out her hand. This was business, wasn't it? Maybe she wasn't paying him, but he was doing her a service, and she'd find ways—meals and whatever else she could think of—to at least make some of his time up to him.

His mouth curved ever so subtly, like he understood the clear dismissal, but it amused him rather than frustrated him. He took her hand in his, shook, but didn't let go.

"I'll be back tomorrow to look through the rest of your research," he said.

Kate could scarcely concentrate on the words with her hand completely engulfed in his. A heat so incongruent to the cold winter night around them.

He released her hand back into the cold. "But I'm staying right here until you're safely inside."

She rolled her eyes, though she didn't…hate that he was being a gentleman. It was like someone caring about her. She knew he didn't. He was basically a stranger. This was common courtesy or something.

But even that was rare in her life.

"Bye, Brody," she said, turning away and marching toward the office building.

"Bye, Kate."

AFTER WATCHING KATE walk quickly to the smaller building where her office was located, and arguing himself into his truck rather than going back inside and demanding to drive her home, Brody drove back to the ranch.

It didn't sit right. Something about little Kate Phillips spending the night out at that old fort in the middle of *nowhere* felt beyond wrong. Unsafe.

You're not in Chicago, and you're not in charge of her.

But she'd seemed…resigned to be this lonely, solitary figure. When she was so…so… Well, he couldn't quite figure out what she was just yet. Probably best if he didn't, and just focused on the task at hand. Helping her figure out what happened to her dad.

He had a lead. A line to tug. That was the only thing he needed to be concerned with.

The snow increased and by the time Brody made it to the ranch, he was glad he'd left when he had. Of course, if he'd waited, he'd be stuck there, and Kate wouldn't be out there all alone.

He scowled at himself. He didn't need to go saving every damsel in distress. Or he'd end up like Jake with a bullet to the gut.

He parked, walked through the blustery snow, stomped his boots on the mats outside, then stepped into warmth.

Home, something inside of him whispered. Cozy glow, the low drone of voices from the kitchen. His family—not the one he'd been born to, but the one that had been forged in the heat and danger of a Middle Eastern desert.

He took off his winter gear, hanging and putting everything carefully away, not because he was so inherently clean, but because he'd quickly learned if he didn't he'd have damp boots and layers the next morning when the chores needed to be done.

He stepped into the kitchen. Everyone, including Zara, was huddled around the small farmhouse table. They needed a bigger one, and good Lord, they needed someone who could cook something beyond frozen dinners.

He had a sneaking suspicion Zara was more of a cook than she let on, but had no desire to feed all of them.

The pan of frozen lasagna looked like it had been through a battle of its own. Only a small sliver remained.

He was inherently thankful Kate had included vegetables in his meal.

"Better get in here quick if you're going to get any," Landon offered. Tech expert and the only one of them who grinned or joked with any regularity, Landon often acted as the face of the Thompson brothers, when Cal's uptight frowning didn't fare well.

"Already ate," Brody returned.

"You did? Where?" Cal demanded.

"Did you need my minute-by-minute itinerary, Sergeant?"

Cal scowled. As that hadn't been his real rank even when they had been deployed and active Team Breaker members.

There was the scrape of chairs, mutterings about things to do. Zara helped Jake to his feet. He was still hobbling, but he was looking better. Getting better. And he had the pretty little ranch hand to nurse him back to health.

Brody didn't know why that seemed *lucky*.

Brody certainly wasn't lucky, because after two minutes it was clear to see everyone had deserted him so Cal could lecture him.

Brody found he didn't have the stomach for it tonight. So he thought he'd cut it off at the pass. "Cal, I get it. I'm not doing this to make you mad."

"Aren't you?" Cal still sat at the table. Brody wondered if his father had been the normal sort if this might remind him of a teenage dressing down. Was Cal the kind of father figure Brody would have wanted if they weren't all about the same age?

No easy answer for that. But there was for Cal's question.

He grinned. "Just an enjoyable happenstance."

Cal snorted.

"They took us out," Brody said, low and letting some of his frustration simmer through. He gripped the ancient kitchen counter, needing something to steady himself where he was. "They plopped us in the middle of nowhere."

"To keep us alive, Brody."

"Sure, but did we sign up for erasing our old lives to keep us alive? I didn't. I signed up for helping people. Now, I don't have a death wish, particularly at the hands of some terrorist lowlife, so I'm happy to be here, laying low, but I can't… She needs help. An easy kind of help. An easy kind of help I happen to excel at."

"You're already in the paper. You want every townsperson with a problem to solve to come to you?"

"Sure, why not?"

Cal groaned.

"I didn't sign up for this life. I'll accept it, but I won't turn my back on people who could use my help. That's my line in the sand. It should be yours, too." And because if he stayed he'd only get madder, Brody turned and left Cal to do the dishes on his own.

Zara was coming down the stairs as he approached the bottom.

"Headed home?"

She shook her head. "Probably stay."

"You ever not here?" he asked, meaning for it to come out like a joke, but he still had a little bit more edge in his voice thanks to Cal, so it landed all wrong.

She paused on the stairs, blocking his way up. "Rarely. You got a problem with that?"

Brody sighed, feeling like a jerk. "No, I don't."

"Good." But she didn't move. She frowned down at him. "You know, Kate shouldn't..." She shifted, uncomfortably, something he rarely saw from Zara, who always seemed so sure of herself. "If you want a space to work, Kate shouldn't feel like it can't be here."

"That's exactly what she seemed to feel like. Wonder why?" Brody had no idea why he was standing up for Kate. He'd known Zara longer. Hell, he *liked* Zara. But Zara was so...strong, and Kate was all alone.

Zara's entire demeanor changed, she charged forward, brushing past him to get off the stairs. "You don't know anything, Brody. Keep that in mind."

"I know one thing, Zara. She seems like she could use a friend, and she doesn't have one. You, on the other hand, have plenty." Brody didn't watch to see if that comment hit its mark. It was none of his business, anyway.

One of these damn days, he'd learn how to mind his own.

Chapter Five

Kate whistled to herself as she made a quick microwave oatmeal breakfast. The snow would be enough to keep everyone away this morning—visitors, Mr. Field. Everyone would be hunkered down or shoveling out.

And she got a morning to herself at the fort to enjoy. Lonely? Maybe, but at least today she was alone with a lot of things she loved.

After she shoveled the walks, she'd finish the new exhibit, maybe digitize some of the records for the fort's website. She'd have all that history all to herself, and *that* was something to whistle about.

As she set to walk back to the office building with her oatmeal, the sun was finally beginning to peek its way above the mountains. Kate tramped through the snow around the back of the buildings where she could get a better view. Maybe stand in the cold, eat her warm oatmeal and watch the sunrise.

Gorgeous. She almost felt content, but as the light began trailing over the world around her, she saw something odd.

Snowmobile tracks. That went all the way up to the

office building she'd slept in. Weird. Maybe Mr. Field had come by last night and forgotten his key? But surely he would have seen her car in the lot and known she'd stayed over. Surely he would have knocked.

Kate pulled her phone out of her pocket and checked for messages. If he'd snowmobiled all the way out here in the dark, come straight to the office building rather than the main building, wouldn't he have tried to contact her?

She looked around the vast gorgeous white of a Wyoming winter, and felt a shudder of unease, no matter how beautiful the sunrise was.

Silly, of course. Thinking about her father's disappearance always gave her that paranoid watched feeling. But she couldn't enjoy the sunrise now, so she turned and headed back for the front door.

Which she'd left unlocked when she headed over to the main building. She stopped in her tracks. If someone had come out this way, they could be in there now.

Don't do this to yourself again.

Kate closed her eyes and focused on her breathing. She wouldn't go back to being that girl she'd been when Dad first disappeared. She could not allow herself to fall back into those old fearful traps that made her miserable.

"Kate."

She screamed. Then immediately winced when she recognized the voice. She didn't want to open her eyes and face the owner of that voice, but she could hardly run away. She sighed and opened her eyes.

"Are you okay?" Brody asked, concern etched all over his face.

Kate tried to smile, but she knew it failed. "Of course. You just scared me is all."

"I thought you would have heard me come up."

She couldn't have possibly heard anything over the heavy pounding of her heart. "Lost in thought. Pretty morning." She gestured to the sun, the mountains far off in the distance.

Brody looked, but she saw him take in the snowmobile tracks, the footprints. He studied the landscape with a cold assessing stare that left her mesmerized for a second.

Then he moved forward so swiftly she didn't have a chance to ask him what he was doing before he took her by the arm and started pulling her toward the front. "Come inside, Kate."

She didn't argue with him. Didn't know why or what he was even doing. He wrenched open the door and muttered about small towns and locking doors.

"What on earth?"

"What on earth is right? What's going on around here?"

"Well, I was trying to eat my oatmeal and watch the sunrise."

"And presumably found those snowmobile tracks, the footprints of at least three people and yet you were still standing outside in an open field, all while the door to shelter and possible safety is unlocked."

Kate blinked. *Three* sets of footprints? She hadn't

really thought they'd be...different people's footprints. But that still didn't mean... It couldn't mean...

Kate cleared her throat and tried to look imperious. "There are quite a few explanations if you'd like to listen to them instead of overreact."

He looked taken aback. "I do *not* overreact."

"Could have fooled me."

He gaped at her, and she couldn't fight back a smile. She'd made a man like Brody Thompson speechless? Not a bad way to start the day.

"It was probably Mr. Field. I'll call later to make sure, but he often comes by just that way. And he's the forgetful sort. If Hazeleigh wasn't here to keep him organized, he probably forgot his keys. Or maybe he got distracted. You can never tell with him."

"You were scared," Brody pointed out, his voice oddly flat.

"I was...jumpy. Digging into my father's disappearance always makes me jumpy. But I'm safe here."

She had to be.

"Three sets of prints isn't one Mr. Field."

"Would you like me to be scared?" she returned, with a little too much snap to her tone, considering Brody was helping her. She took a deep breath and struggled to find a smile. "Look, it's fine. I promise. I'm fine. Why are you here?"

"To look through the rest of your research. I told you I'd be back."

"I know, I just assumed with the snow... The roads couldn't have been good."

He shoved his hands deep into his pockets. "They weren't so bad."

She didn't believe him, but she also couldn't figure out why he would have braved the roads to help her. But here he was. Maybe he was just a man who really felt committed to following through.

"I appreciate your dedication," she said, maybe a tad primly.

"Do you store anything valuable here?"

She resisted the urge to roll her eyes since he clearly was determined not to let it go. "Probably not in the way you mean. We have one-of-a-kind documents and artifacts, but not the type that are going to go for big bucks. Trust me, it was Mr. Field, or maybe some lost hikers looking for shelter. There's nothing here anyone could want."

Brody looked down at the crates of research she'd spent ten years compiling. "You so sure about that?"

Kate's stomach sank.

BRODY WASN'T PROUD of himself. She went pale right there before him.

What was it about people who couldn't lock their damn doors? People bound and determined to let threats get the better of them, rather than fight them off at the first sign.

"I've…been doing this for ten years. I've talked to every cop, every private detective in a fifty-mile radius. Nothing in here has ever given anyone any clue where he might have gone. What he might have done."

"You don't know what Stanley Music is."

"It's a music company!" she practically yelled. "There are *invoices* with an address and phone number. It made all the sense in the world."

"Invoices." Brody frowned and thought over everything he'd gone through yesterday. "I didn't see any invoices."

"They were with the credit card statements. I paper clipped everything together. Any receipts or invoices that went with the charges. They were there."

"There were no invoices with the statements. Not for Stanley anyway."

"You're wrong." She straightened her shoulders, temper giving her pallor some color in her cheeks. She turned on a heel and marched back to her office.

Brody followed, leaving a healthy distance between them. He'd been through everything in the finance pile. Not everything entirely. It was possible she'd misplaced something, but Kate didn't strike him as the careless type.

She began to flip through the files. Finding the one she wanted, opening it, pulling out the credit card statements. She flipped through all the receipts and invoices clipped to the first. Then the second. Then the third, with increasingly jerky movements.

"I can't find them. I must have… I must have done something with them." She took a slow steadying breath, clearly trying to keep from panicking. But it was there in her eyes, darting around the office. "I'll just have to go through everything. It'll be there."

She blew out a breath, very slowly, very carefully. "I must have misplaced them. Left them somewhere. You might have put them in a different file with your organizing. They're…" She spoke softly, almost to herself. But then on another deep breath in and out, she looked up at him. "They *were* here."

"I believe you," he said, both because he did and because she seemed to need the reassurance. "Let's spread it all out again. Check the room I was in."

She nodded her head, a little bit too vigorously.

They spent hours going through every folder, every last shred of paper. Brody took a break to go pick them up some food from town. She didn't touch her sandwich except the few times he'd remind her to take a bite.

The single-minded focus she had made him a little uncomfortable, because it bordered on…well, a lot of behaviors that weren't conducive to solving a problem. But she wasn't in the military. She didn't have to worry about personal investment—this was her life. Her father. It *was* personal, and he couldn't tell her to be calm or detach herself from it.

He'd have to take that on for her.

After they got through all her files, she tore her office apart. Sure they must have fallen behind a drawer, or desk, or got stuck in a book.

"Maybe they're at home," she said, sitting in the middle of her little office, the entire contents all but exploded around her. "They must be. They have to be."

Brody thought about her compact car and all that snow. The plows had been out, but the roads were still bad. It was clear she wouldn't rest until she could check her home, but Brody was pretty sure they were gone.

And she was going to have to deal with that, but not until she was ready. "I can drive you."

She started to try to put her office to rights, then stopped abruptly. "No. No, this is insane. I'm letting you make me insane."

He didn't point out it was hardly his fault her invoices were missing. She was teetering on the verge of a meltdown. He was impressed she hadn't fallen off that edge yet, but he was pretty sure any commentary from him would push her.

"I can't do this again," she muttered to herself. "I won't."

"Do what?"

She looked up at him, blinked as if surprised to find him actually there. "Nothing. It's not important." She sucked in a breath. "I mean, this is just an overreaction. Clearly they got misplaced. What other possibility is there?"

"Snowmobile tracks, unknown footprints, you don't lock doors out here apparently."

She looked at him, mouth hanging slightly open. "You think someone *stole* them?"

"I think someone *could* have stolen them."

"They went through my things, stole just these, what was it, three invoices? Out of all those papers? All that work?"

"Maybe the three invoices were the only incriminating thing."

"This is insane. No, I'm sorry. I can't get on board with that. I appreciate your help, Brody, I do. And when I'm home next, I'll check out my room. I'm almost certain they're there. It will all check out and..." She was getting ahold of herself, but it was a hard-won thing. "I can't let myself do this again. I have to let it go." She wrapped her arms around herself, continuing to nod. "I finally have to let it go."

"You want to just give up?" Brody asked, surprised that would be her go to. He didn't think it'd last, but to even try to give it up seemed incongruous to everything she'd ever done up to this point.

She let her arms fall and began cleaning up again. Bustling around busily. "Like I said, I really appreciate the help, but it was a..." She stopped, clearly trying to come up with a word. "Well, I appreciate the help. I'm sure you have more important ranch work to be doing."

She was dismissing him. Brody laughed, maybe with too much of an edge to it, but if there was one thing that got under his skin, it was people not taking the proper precautions. "You are not staying here alone."

She stopped what she was doing, straightened. "I beg your pardon."

"Call Mr. Field."

She fisted her hands on her hips. "Don't take that tone with me."

"Call Mr. Field and ask him if that was his snowmobile. His *three* sets of footprints. Your father disappeared, Kate. Maybe you and the town would like to believe that was voluntary. Hell, maybe it was, but I know when things aren't right. Things aren't right."

"You are paranoid," she whispered, like a shocked accusation.

"You aren't paranoid enough."

"No, I went down that particular road. I played that game, and…" She shook her head violently and squeezed her eyes shut. "This is too much," she muttered to herself. Eyes opened, she stared him down. "Brody, I appreciate your help, but I can't… My father left. I didn't handle that very well when it first happened. I thought everyone was out to get me. I thought I was being followed. I had a very bad year or two, but—"

Everything inside of him stilled. "Someone was following you when you were sixteen?"

"That isn't what I said. I said I *thought* someone was. I was delusional—with grief, and worry, and all sorts of things. I was alone and unbalanced. I would have gone to a therapist, but my mother said I would be fine if I just let it all go."

"You didn't," Brody pointed out, gesturing to all her work.

She surveyed the mess, and just looked so sad. "I tried. It took a while to create some balance. No, I didn't fully let it go, but I stopped letting it rule my life. I can't go back to that."

"And I can't walk away from this knowing you might very well be in danger."

Chapter Six

Kate wasn't sure how long she stood, staring at Brody with her mouth hanging open. She hadn't been sure what she'd be getting when she asked for Brody's help, but definitely, *definitely* not this.

"You…must be joking."

"Why would I be joking?"

"Why would I be in *danger*?"

He sighed, as if she were a child who couldn't understand a very complex problem. And he didn't have the words to explain it. "I'm well versed in analyzing situations, acknowledging threats and picking up on cues that danger—"

"How?"

He clamped his mouth shut for a moment, stood there looking like something frozen. Then he scowled. "Trust me."

Which seemed like the most absurd thing to say. Trust? A man she barely knew who was just supposed to be helping her *research* her father's disappearance. "Why?"

"Are you always this difficult?"

"No. I'm very rarely difficult. I am biddable, and normal. This is not normal. This is… You need to leave now."

His expression didn't really change. It…melted. Or just…blanked. There was nothing there now except a very stoic man blocking her exit.

Kate swallowed, not sure what her next move would be if he refused, but eventually he let his crossed arms fall.

"Fine," he said.

"So, you're going?"

He turned and began walking away. "Not exactly."

Not exactly. Kate scrambled after him. He was already opening the door to the building.

"What do you mean *not exactly*?" she called after him.

He stopped and turned. "I'll sit in my truck if you don't want me in here. But I'm not going anywhere as long as you're determined to be all alone, in the middle of nowhere, with three people snooping around where you slept last night. Alone. Without any damn protection."

Then he let the door close behind him, leaving Kate with the echo of a door slam and complete and utter disbelief.

"I am not in any danger," she muttered to herself. How could she be in danger? There had been years she'd pored herself into this. Nothing had disappeared. No strange men, no cops, no private investigators had noticed the Stanley Music thing. They'd had the invoices.

And who would have looked into those? Kate herself hadn't, because it made *sense*. Maybe they were missing, but it still made sense Dad would have spent money at a music company.

Someone was following you when you were sixteen?

It had been her imagination. Everyone had said so. And nothing had ever happened to her, so they were right. They were right and Brody was… Well, he was overstepping.

Brody was off base. Maybe something was wrong with him. Maybe Zara had sent him here to mess with her. Okay, that was a bit far-fetched. Maybe Zara had stopped being her friend, but even angry Kate couldn't imagine Zara being *mean*.

He needed to…back off. Go away. Most certainly not stick around. She had to go tell him to leave. Make it clear.

She grabbed her coat and walked outside. It was snowing again, which meant she'd have to spend the night here again. Now, thanks to Brody being a *lunatic*, that thought left her with dread.

No, he did not get to ruin her peace of mind *and* sit out there in the parking lot like some kind of misplaced babysitter.

He'd be a really hot babysitter.

That unbidden thought made her even madder as she marched up to his truck and knocked on his window. He looked up, rolled the window down with a pleasant smile on his face. "Help you?"

"I could call the police."

"And tell them what?"

"That an insane person is insisting I not be alone. You're…you're stalking me!"

He grinned. "I'm just sitting in my truck in a parking lot, Kate."

She opened her mouth to say something to him, but she had nothing. *Nothing.* He was just going to sit here. Even if she called the cops?

"What is wrong with you?" she demanded.

He shrugged. "I get it. You feel like I'm overreacting. But I don't feel like I am, and if something happened to you because I went home like you demanded, well, I wouldn't be able to forgive myself. I'm sorry if that puts a wrench in your life, but I plan on only doing things I can live with for the rest of mine."

Which kind of insinuated there'd been a time and place when he'd done something he wasn't living very comfortably with. She almost softened toward him, even knowing she shouldn't. She really shouldn't.

"I can drive you home," he said earnestly. "I can drive you to Hazeleigh's and you could stay with her until the roads are clear and she can drive you back here. I can do a lot of things, but I can't leave you alone when everything I've observed tells me there's a high statistical chance you or your information is a target of some kind."

"You sound like a cop."

His easy smile didn't fade, but something in his eyes shuttered. "I'm not."

If he drove her back to Mom's, she'd need someone to drive her back to the fort for work tomorrow. But she'd have time to look for those invoices.

You know they're not there.

She sighed, the snow swirling heavily around her.

She did know that. She was very careful not to take things back to the house that Mom might find and get upset about. She was very careful to keep everything together and organized. She was very careful.

Those invoices were missing. "I don't understand how or why someone would have taken three slips of paper. Even if they were incriminating. How?"

"I don't quite know, Kate. But I'll help you find out."

He seemed so earnest. So competent. No one ever wanted to help her find out *anything*. She knew she should be smart and resist it, but she just wasn't strong enough to do that.

"All right. Let me call Hazeleigh and make sure she's..." Kate trailed off as Brody's smile deepened. "You already talked to her."

"Just as a precaution."

A precaution. He was unhinged. She was going to get in his car and let him drive her places? She sighed. "I've got to get my things. I'll be right back," she muttered.

BRODY WAS QUITE pleased with himself. Less pleased with the way the snowfall kept increasing. When Kate reappeared with a backpack and a purse, she was covered in snow by the time she jogged from the building to his truck.

She clambered in, tossed the bags in the back. "Going to get bad again."

Brody eyed the sky, the quickly disappearing parking lot around him. "Looks like." He reversed out of the parking spot, his windshield wipers going at full blast. "Did you ever call Mr. Field?"

"No."

"Afraid of the truth?"

He couldn't look at her to parse her reaction. His eyes had to stay on the road—if what little he could see would be considered a road. They hadn't gone a mile when he'd regretted his decision.

"Brody, this is bad."

"Yeah." Whiteout bad. "I'm thinking I should probably just turn back and we both stay in your little office building tonight?"

"Yes, but be careful. You don't want to get stuck in a di—"

There was the squeal of tires, Brody barely caught it over the roar of the wind. He couldn't see anything, but he felt the impact. Someone had crashed into them. They jerked forward. Brody tried to slam on the brakes, but they got bumped again, so even though he had his foot stomped on the brake, they went forward on the slick road.

Brody kept a death grip on the steering wheel, but the truck was skidding. No, it wasn't skidding—it was being *pushed.* Whatever car had run into them was still trying to drive forward? Whoever had hit them must have lost consciousness with their foot on the gas? Or maybe were so confused by the storm, didn't know to stop.

Or...

Brody didn't let his mind immediately go to nefarious, purposeful crashes. In a whiteout like this, an accident was all but inevitable. But he'd still take precautions. With his foot still on the brake, he tried to see what was going on.

He couldn't see anything. Not headlights, but maybe the slight outline of another truck? He had to bring his focus back to his windshield. The other truck was pushing his truck from the side. If he hit the gas, maybe he could dislodge them from the truck trying to push them off the road. They'd risk skidding in the snowy conditions, but Brody figured he could handle that best.

Kate was being too quiet, but he had to get them to safety before he could risk looking at her.

"Hold on," he said. He punched the gas, and the tires squealed, but they didn't propel forward.

They were stuck. In the snow, or maybe ice underneath. There was no way to get out of this. He heard the crunch of metal and then *thankfully* the other vehicle seemed to reverse and hopefully—

Another painful jerk of the car, metal screeching. A purposeful, painful ram that sent the truck tipping into a ditch.

"Hold on," Brody yelled as the truck fell—hard, and mostly on its side. Glass shattered as something impaled the driver's side window. Brody managed to hunch forward to avoid being skewered himself, though he felt something scrape against his back, pain searing with it.

White was all around them, pain radiating down his back. Brody struggled to unbuckle himself with his limited range of mobility. He could see what had impaled his truck window—a twisted, rusted mile marker made of metal.

He swore, viciously, because the narrow miss left his bones feeling a little jellied. Swearing, breathing, acting brought his composure back.

He looked at Kate. She was hanging limply, the seat belt the only thing that had kept her from falling into his seat. A little trickle of blood dripped from her chin.

Brody swore again as he leaped into action. He struggled with his seat belt—eventually pulling the pocketknife from his pocket and cutting the straps off. He wouldn't be able to get out of his door, so they'd have to get out of Kate's.

"Kate…."

"Hurts," she muttered.

"I just bet. Can you open your eyes?"

She groaned, but eventually blinked her eyes open. They widened, in surprise or understanding. "Brody."

"Can you get your door open?"

She winced, closed her eyes again, but kept moving. Turning toward her door. She managed to pull the handle and push the door open, but it only immediately fell back closed.

Brody tried to leverage himself closer. "Try again," he said, gritting his teeth against the pain in his back and the discomfort from contorting his body this way.

She did as she was told, and he managed to hold it open this time. "Okay, climb out if you can."

She struggled, first to get her buckle undone, then to get up and over and onto the ground. Brody's arm was shaking by the time she was finally free of the door. He had to drop it, let it slam shut.

Swearing, he gave his arm a bit of a rest by trying

to gather up everything he would need. He grabbed the gun from the glove compartment, made sure the safety was on, and then shoved it in his pocket. Cal was going to be *all* kinds of ticked off about the truck, but Brody figured he had to survive this before he worried about Cal's anger.

He reached into the back and pulled out Kate's bags. Who knew what they were going to do next, but it might pay to have whatever she had packed away on them. He shoved the door open, and tossed the bags out.

Kate was standing, but bent over like she couldn't quite handle being upright. Still, when she heard him grunt, she looked up, then shuffled through the snow to reach out and hold the door open so he could get himself free of the truck.

He let out a vicious streak of curses as the pain worked its way through his body, and seemed to stiffen every last inch of him. But he looked at Kate. She had a nasty knot on her temple with blood dripping from it.

She must have knocked her head on the door when they'd been run into. "I don't suppose you have a first-aid kit in your bags?"

"No," she said, shaking her head, but the movement had her knees buckling.

Brody managed to scoop her up before she fell to the ground. "Gotcha."

"Dizzy," she grumbled.

"Yeah, concussions'll do that."

Brody looked around. The world was white. The wind howled and the snow kept falling. There was no sign of anyone. There weren't even tire tracks because the snow had already covered them up. He couldn't ask anyone to come out in this. Even emergency services would struggle in this mess.

"We'll have to walk back to the fort. I don't even think we got a mile down the road, so it's doable." He wished he were dressed a little better for the weather, but he'd manage.

"You can't carry me," Kate mumbled into his shoulder.

"Of course I can." He'd carried his brother Dunne farther, when Dunne had been seriously injured in a dust storm. He could carry a petite woman in the snow.

He just had to make sure he knew which way they were going. Where they were. He pulled the pocketknife from his pocket again. He had a little compass on the center of it. They'd been traveling westbound on the road, but he couldn't *see* the road.

"Brody, I can stand."

"I can carry you. You don't happen to know which way we need to go, do you?"

She turned her head, then groaned and closed her eyes.

He'd take that as a no. He scooped up her bags, hissed a little as he slung them over his shoulder and the straps hit the scrape on his back. He studied the truck. It would mostly be facing the direction they'd been driving. Maybe a little off course, but if he could find the road at the back of the truck, he could shuffle along and follow it as best he could back to the fort.

The road *had* been plowed, so there wasn't as much snow on it. All he had to do was follow that edge along the plowed snowbank.

"You just hang tight," Brody murmured, when Kate tried to mumble something, but it didn't sound like actual words. "We'll get you warm and all fixed up."

He'd have to find a way.

Chapter Seven

It was cold. Bitterly, bitterly cold. Her face hurt. Her temple *really* hurt. Her arms hurt from clutching Brody's neck. Her entire body hurt from being rammed and jostled.

She couldn't open her eyes. Every time she did, a wave of nausea went through her and she thought she might throw up right there on Brody's shirt.

So she kept her eyes shut. And tried to keep her mind blank, but all she could think was…

He was walking them to their death. He wasn't *from* here. He clearly didn't know anything about survival. They should have hunkered down in the truck. There was heat there, even if they had crashed into a ditch.

How had they crashed into a ditch? She understood someone had run into them—though it was some kind of bad odds to have a car accident in a blizzard in the middle of nowhere—but where had the other vehicle gone?

She played it back. It was fuzzy. She was pretty sure she'd passed out for a little bit, which was beyond terrifying. She'd never really had anything wrong with her. She'd never even broken a limb. Never been put under anesthesia.

And she'd lost consciousness over a bump to the head. "Going to die."

"Don't be dramatic," Brody said, and he sounded so…sure. So strong. Even as the cold air soaked deeper and her whole body throbbed with aches and pains, and she was certain he couldn't be walking in the right direction, that certainty in his voice soothed her.

Maybe he *did* know what he was doing.

Wouldn't that be funny?

"There we are."

She managed to open her eyes, though it was a hard-won thing, like her eyelashes had frozen together. All she saw was white. Even Brody was covered in white.

"Impending death?"

"Ha. Ha," he replied, though she hadn't really been making a joke.

Then she saw it. The flagpole. Right in front of her face. Brody moved around it and she saw the lump she was pretty sure was her car, because there was a little antenna coming up out of it.

"I'm dreaming. Hallucinating. Psychotic breaking."

"You are fine," Brody said through gritted teeth. "Aside from being a little overwrought."

She laughed, which she supposed proved his point. "Overwrought. Of *course* I'm overwrought. I have invoices missing and people stalking me and you, *you* some stranger I barely know, insisting on helping me and instead getting us into an accident."

"*I* did not get us into an accident. Keys?"

"What about keys?"

"Keys to the building, Kate."

Keys. Keys? "Oh, keys. Purse. But I didn't..."

He set her very carefully on her feet, and he didn't let her go. He positioned her so she was still leaning against him. Which was good, because she couldn't seem to find her balance. The world kept tilt-a-whirling around. She had to close her eyes to make it stop.

She heard the howl of the wind. Felt the cold sink deeper and deeper now that she wasn't all pressed up to Brody's warm body, and wasn't that a shame.

"Kate."

"I want to lie down."

"I'm sure you do, but unless you want to freeze to death—not a fun way to go I'm almost certain—you'll stay standing for another few minutes. Now, open your eyes and tell me which key."

On a heavy sigh, she managed to open her eyes. He held her keychain. She looked at the door they were in front of. Main building. Her arms felt heavy, sluggish, but she managed to point to the one in his hand that would open the main building.

He opened the door, still holding her weight, and then once it was open, he scooped her up again.

It was weird because it wasn't the most comfortable position in the world, but it was kind of nice. To rest her head on his shoulder. To know he was going to take care of things.

When was the last time anyone had taken care of anything for her?

He was flipping the light switch back and forth, cursing under his breath.

"You sure swear a lot."

"Yeah, I'll apologize later."

"Must have lost electricity. Happens sometimes during blizzards."

"Fantastic." He muttered some more things under his breath, but she didn't catch them all. Finally, he set her down on a bench. He crouched in front of her, staring her in the eye. "We need to bandage up your head. Get some water in us. Then we'll figure out what to do."

"We should call someone."

"Not until the worst of this is over," Brody replied. "I don't want anyone coming out in this, do you?"

"No, I suppose not."

"First-aid kit?"

"Under the front desk. I'll—"

She tried to stand, but Brody's arm on her shoulder held her still. "I'll get it. You sit tight. Eyes open. Seated upright. Understood."

"Yes, sir," she said, attempting a mock salute but listing a little to the right.

"God help me," Brody muttered, then he turned on his phone flashlight and disappeared behind the desk. He returned with the first-aid kit. He moved quickly, efficiently, like he was used to such things.

He washed out the cut on her wound, murmuring reassurances when she hissed out a breath of pain. Gently, even though his hands were large and rough, he smoothed a bandage over her head where it hurt the worst.

"Water?"

"Mr. Field has a little fridge in his office."

Brody disappeared again, then returned with two bottles of water. He'd already downed half of his and handed her the other one. "Drink some of this. No pain-killers till we know the extent of your concussion."

"I've never had a concussion."

"That's good."

She sipped the water, watched as Brody studied the building. The quiet, the lack of being jostled and the water was a bit like coming back to earth. Her head hurt viciously. Her body was stiff and sore. This was bad, and the full reality of that began to settle on her shoulders.

They were going to have to *do* something.

"The third building," she said, figuring it was their best chance at a warm night, with food, shelter. It would require roughing it, and using the historical artifacts, but it would keep them warm and safe through the night.

"What about it?"

She lifted her hand to touch where her head hurt, but then thought better of it. "It's an old cabin. We use it for living history and demonstrations. We can build a fire. I can heat up water on the stove. There are bed frames and old blankets. Nothing great, but it'll get us through the night. There might even be some supplies to make bread."

"Bread," he echoed.

"You should grab some water, maybe some perish-ables from the fridge. There should be sacks behind the front desk to help carry some things." She tried to stand. He was by her side in a second.

"I'm still dizzy, but I can walk. Really."

Slowly, he released her and she managed to prove her point. She could stand on her own, take a few steps. He studied her for a good minute before he apparently decided to be satisfied.

"All right. Don't move. Don't carry anything. You don't want to mess around with a concussion. Just stand here until I get everything ready."

Kate agreed, and then had to swallow down the lump in her throat. *Get everything ready.* He'd carried her through a *blizzard.* She didn't know what to do with any of it, but she knew she owed him...everything.

BRODY GRABBED ANYTHING he thought might be useful overnight. They were quickly losing whatever light could be found amidst all that snow, and he wanted to get settled—not just so Kate could rest, but so he could fortify this building they'd be staying in against whatever threat might be out there.

Someone had knocked them into that ditch. It might have been the middle of a blizzard, but Brody knew what it was like to be under attack. What it meant to be a target.

Somehow, Kate had become a target. After ten years—no, she'd said weird stuff had happened in those first years before she'd backed off. She must have been close then, and he was close now.

Brody wouldn't have thought a small town in Wyoming would be the kind of place threats and purposeful accidents would happen, but he also hadn't expected dead bodies and murder—which they'd dealt with earlier in the month, leading to Jake's gunshot wound.

Bad things could happen anywhere, and when people did bad things, they often went to great lengths to cover them up.

Brody returned to where he'd left Kate. She was far too pale, but she was still standing. Her eyes were focused and open now. She definitely had a concussion, of that Brody had no doubt. But she didn't seem to have any other serious issues beyond bumps and scrapes and bruises.

He wouldn't be able to carry her *and* the supplies over to the other building—not because he was incapable, but because he simply didn't have the right kind of bags to transport everything in and keep his hands free enough to carry her.

"Why don't you wait here while I—"

She shook her head, then winced and pressed a palm to her forehead. "I'm not saying I'm great. But I can walk over to the cabin."

He didn't like it, but it was either that or leave her alone, and he didn't like that either. He hadn't seen a sign of anyone on the long hike over, but that didn't mean threats weren't looming.

"Okay. Lead the way."

"I can carry—"

"I'll carry everything," he said firmly. "You get us there."

She didn't seem satisfied, but eventually she clasped her hands together. "Okay."

Brody grabbed her bags he'd carried from the truck, the bags of food, first aid and water bottles he'd taken from this building, then followed her back into the cold, blinding white.

He hadn't realized how damn cold that wind was until he'd been out of it.

He waited for her to lock the door, then looked to where the third cabin would be. He couldn't see it in the white—not really.

"We just walk straight," she yelled over the howling wind. "Stay right behind me. We get turned around, we're in trouble."

Brody wasn't too worried about it. He could find things in worse conditions than this, but he let her feel like she was in some charge. He followed her slow shuffling steps, biting back the frustration both at the slow pace and how much pain she must be in. He had to repeatedly talk himself out of dropping his bags, scooping her up and getting her to that cabin himself.

But they finally reached the building, covered in white until Kate brushed snow from the padlock, undid it and then shoved the door open. She waved him inside, but he nudged her in front of him.

He closed the door behind him and looked around. Too dark to make out much of anything. He put the bags on the ground, pulled out his phone for a flashlight.

"Point it this way," Kate said, moving his arm to angle the light toward what he supposed was a kind of…kitchen. She began to move around the cabin and it took him a few minutes to realize she was lighting old-fashioned lanterns. Then she knelt next to the big hearth in the middle of the room and began to work at starting a fire.

Eventually, she'd filled the place with enough light they could move around and see well enough. It was a big open space, though different areas had clearly been made into the kitchen, bedroom, living room. There was furniture, but all old. Probably historically accurate.

They were protected from the wind, but the place was still cold. Though warmer if he stood closer to the fire.

He needed to do a bit of a perimeter check, bolster the doors. But he wanted to be sure she wasn't going to collapse on him before he left her alone for even a second.

"Why don't you sit down," he said as she continued to putter around the cabin. Hell, she'd filled a big kettle with snow and now had it boiling on the old stove. "Rest a little."

"Are you going to sit down and rest a little?"

"I don't have a concussion."

She wrinkled her nose at that. "Do you know anything about concussions?"

"Enough. You don't want to push yourself." He pulled the rocking chair from the corner to be next to the fire and pointed at her to sit. "If you haven't developed any new symptoms in a few hours, you can take some painkillers if you've got the right kind. Maybe we should eat something."

She sat gingerly. "Didn't you get hurt at all?"

"Just a few scrapes," he replied. "I'll get you a snack

and some water and—" He turned to go to where he'd left the bags, but she leaped to her feet.

"You're bleeding."

He waved her off. "I'm fine."

"Brady, that's an awful gash." She grabbed his arm in an attempt to keep him still. She peered at his back. "It cut through your coat, your clothes, your *skin*. You have to let me clean and bandage it for you."

He tried to twist his head enough to see, but it was across his back. He doubted it was as bad as she thought—he'd survived quite a bit worse—but it probably would be best to get it cleaned up. Infections were no fun—he'd dealt with his share of those too.

"For heaven's sake. You sit your butt down and let me put something on that." She gave him a little shove toward the rocking chair, but he stayed firm. There were things to do—protections to make.

"I am serious, Brody. I will..." She looked around the room, clearly looking for some kind of suitable threat. "I'll tie you to that chair if I have to," she said. Seriously. As if she could.

He shook his head. "No, you won't."

"After you fell asleep, I could—"

"I'm not saying you can't. I'm saying you won't. But if it means that much to you..." He walked over to the chair. Sat down, angled so his back was to her rather than the back of the chair. "Bandage away."

She scowled at him, but went to the bags and found the first-aid kit. She stood behind him and studied his back for a moment. "You're going to have to take off your coat, and shirt, and everything," she said at length.

He shrugged out of his coat, pulled his sweatshirt and thermal up over his head. When she did nothing, said nothing, he looked over his shoulder at her.

She was staring at his back with a kind of wide-eyed shock he didn't think meant his injury was *that* bad. She didn't look horrified, or even scared.

She looked interested.

He tried not to grin to himself. "Is it that bad?"

She startled a little. "Oh, no. Probably not. I mean, it's bad." She bustled over to the stove. "I need to wash it up a bit before I disinfect it." She started carrying the kettle back over to them and the fire.

He jumped to his feet. "You shouldn't be—"

"I feel much better. Really. My head hurts, and I feel a little nauseous, but my vision isn't fuzzy anymore. I don't feel that dizzy. Sit."

He frowned at her, but she was…lucid, moving fine, capable, and it would probably be best if he was bandaged up. He sat.

She got to work. She had some kind of towel—he hoped from this century instead of the last—and poured the water on it, then began washing his back.

The room got very quiet. He could still hear the howl of the blizzard outside, but they were insulated. The fire was doing its job and warming them up.

"You…have a lot of scars," Kate murmured, the whisper of her breath floating along the bare skin of his back.

Uh-oh.

Uncomfortable with that and the way she touched

said scars so gently, Brody had to fight back the urge to shrug her hands off him. “Yeah, so?”

“What from?”

“Life, Kate.” A life that had never been as kind and gentle as she was being.

“I imagine this will be another one. It might need stitches. I don’t really know…”

“Just bandage it up for now. It’ll be fine. I’m sure of it.”

She sighed, her breath once again moving over him, having a very unfortunate reaction. He tried to think about anything else. The gaps in the plank floor. The way the windowpanes rattled. Someone lived here, without electricity or a phone, over a hundred years ago.

She smoothed the bandages—she had to use more than one due to the length of the cut apparently—and Brody kept his eyes focused on that gap in the floor between his boots.

“There,” she said, apparently pleased with her efforts. “The worst of it should certainly be over by morning, and then we can call someone and get you to a doctor.”

“I’m sure it’s fine.” He got to his feet—away from her soft gentle hands. He picked up his shirt off the ground. It was dry thanks to the heft of his coat, but there was a bloody rip in the back.

“I don’t suppose you’ve got any large men’s shirts lying around here, do you?” He glanced at her.

She didn’t meet his eyes. Her gaze was fixed straight on his chest. She also did not answer his question. Just stared.

He knew he needed to say something. Pull his shirt

on. Do *something* other than stand here, letting his brain go in directions it absolutely could not. Particularly when she had a bandage on her head and a concussion and…

Yeah, Kate Phillips was off-limits. He pulled his shirt on, trying not to wince as pain lanced his back.

She blinked, finally raising her gaze to meet his. Her cheeks turned an appealing shade of pink.

Do not. Do not. Do not. He cleared his throat, stepped back. "I'm going to check the perimeter."

Chapter Eight

He disappeared before she could think of anything to say. Out into the howling white.

"Check the perimeter." Long after Brody had disappeared, Kate found herself saying those words out loud. Over and over again. Who said *check the perimeter?* What was there to check?

She considered it as she tidied up from bandaging him. She fretted a bit about the size and depth of that scrape on his back, but that led to thoughts about his back…which led to thoughts about his front.

She blew out a long breath. She had never been that up close and personal with a man's body before. He was just so…big. And strong. And there were all different shapes and sizes of scars—like he'd been to war and back.

That stopped her in her tracks. Maybe he'd been a soldier of some kind. She knew a few guys from her high school class who'd joined the military. It would make sense. But why hadn't he just said that?

Well, perhaps he'd had a terrible time. If he'd seen

combat, perhaps he had PTSD. Poor man. He wanted to avoid the subject and—

She probably should focus on getting through the night and a lot less on Brody Thompson.

She studied the cabin. She wished she had more blankets out here, especially since Brody's coat was torn. And bloody. But if they took turns and kept the fire going through the night, surely someone could come dig them out by morning.

Brody's poor truck might be totaled, which was going to be a problem of its own. But his problem, not hers. Though she should probably offer…something? He'd been driving her. But only because he'd insisted. *She* would have stayed put if he hadn't been around… messing with things.

Of course, she'd been the one to approach Brody in the *first* place.

The door swung open and Brody stepped in, once again covered in snow. Though the warmth from the fireplace quickly set to melting it.

"Still going strong. I'm going to have to call my brothers and let them know where I am and convince them we can stay put for the night. You don't think your Mom would try to come get you in this storm, do you?"

Kate was caught so off guard she laughed. When he frowned, she managed to swallow down the rest of her laughter. "Uh, no. She'll just assume I've hunkered down."

"You're not even going to give her a call?"

"No, it won't matter."

He gave her such an aghast kind of look she felt herself explaining even though she didn't want to. "Look, we're not your typical...mother–daughter... I don't live with her because... It's...complicated. She won't be worried about me. The end."

"You sure?"

"Positive." She gave a smile and a nod. Because she was sure, and fine, and that was...her life. "Call your brothers. I'll see what I can put together for dinner."

His eyes darted to her temple, where the bandage was. It ached, throbbed and she doubted she'd be able to sleep tonight if she couldn't take something for the pain, but she really was capable of moving around and doing things.

"Don't worry. I'm fine." *No one ever worries about me, and I am always just fine.*

He seemed to take that at face value and pulled his phone out of his pocket. He walked over to the far corner and greeted his brother. Kate puttered about the kitchen. She had a lot of the ingredients for the different frontier foods she demonstrated making for visitors, but it seemed like a bit much to drag it all out for some ash cake when Brody had grabbed some of the nonperishables she kept in the office. Canned soup over the stove would be the easiest.

"Yeah, look, had a little fender bender so I'm stuck here. I'll have to deal with the truck once it clears up. I'll keep you up to date," Brody was saying into his phone. When she glanced at him, he rolled his eyes and mimed the scolding he was likely receiving from the speaker.

She tried to smile, really, but it was hard to find humor. Truth be told, she would feel pretty good if someone was worried enough about her to yell at her on the phone. She frowned down at the soup.

A few minutes later, she could feel Brody approach. "Soup should be heated through in a few."

He studied the old wood-fire stove she was using. "You know how to do all this pioneer stuff, huh?"

Kate nodded. "I've always liked history, and I always liked the fort. There's an ancestral connection." She shrugged. She didn't really want to see the glazed-over look in his eyes most people got when she talked about history and genealogy. "So, I studied what interested me."

She scooped soup into the replica historical bowls, as the originals were under glass in the museum proper. She carried them over to the rickety table. It felt a little strange to do all of this in her modern clothes, but it was still mostly old hat. "Dad always wanted me to be a history teacher, but this suited me better than trying to wrangle teenagers. I get to live out my prairie fantasies and go home to indoor plumbing and the internet."

"Best of both worlds." He went over to the bags, plucked two bottles of water from them and sat one down in front of her before taking a bowl of soup across from her.

It was…teamwork. It was *strange*. But Brody dug into his soup and it felt kind of…nice. Cozy, almost. Aside from the injuries and what not.

She figured she should keep the conversation going. A pleasant back and forth would make the time pass faster. “Hazeleigh says you were all new to ranching and Zara had to teach you.”

“Mmm. Mostly city boys.”

“So, what brought you to Wyoming?”

“Oh, like I said. Cal’s deal. We just follow.” He waved it off like that was an answer, but it wasn’t much of one. Maybe he thought she’d be bored, like she always assumed people would be bored if she told her stories.

“Were you a soldier before you all decided to ranch?”

His face went very carefully blank, and there was a strange…coldness to his gaze she’d never gotten from him. “Excuse me?”

“I just thought maybe… The scars…and you said *perimeter*.” She stopped herself from stammering out any more explanations. “Never mind.”

“It was a long time ago.”

“Right. Sure. None of my business.” She forced herself to smile at him, then look down at her soup and ate. Eating she could do. And if her mouth was full, she wouldn’t say anything stupid.

After an oppressive silence where it was an effort to swallow past all the discomfort, Brody spoke.

“I was in the army.”

She looked up to meet his gaze over the table. “You don’t have to talk about it. I just… I was trying to make conversation.”

“I know. I just don’t particularly care to relive.”

“Yeah, of course.”

They finished their soup in utter silence, and Kate felt like a moron. This, among all the other reasons why she was a pariah in town, was why she didn't date. Not that this was a date, just that she was bad with people. Conversations. Normality.

She quickly scooped the last bit of soup in her mouth and then stood. "Done?" she asked brightly. "I'll wash up." She reached forward to take his empty bowl, but he grabbed her wrist before she could finish the movement.

His grasp was gentle, but firm enough to anchor her there. "I just…need you not to tell anyone that. The army thing."

She blinked. "It's a secret?"

He seemed to consider that word. "In a way."

"Okay. Sure. Lips are sealed."

He slowly released her wrist, the pads of his fingers trailing down the top of her hand. Did he really have to be *so* good-looking? And did she really have to be so *her*?

NORMALLY, BRODY WOULD have offered to clean up since she'd made dinner, but he needed to do some other things he didn't want her to pay too close attention to. Like setting up signals at all the entrance points. If someone tried to get in through the windows, they'd knock over something that would crash.

"I figured we'd take turns sleeping," she offered, pointing at the "bed" in the corner. Brody had slept in a lot worse conditions, but that still didn't make what he could only assume was a straw mattress a *real* bed.

"Ah, so you *do* believe me about being in danger." He studied the locking mechanism on the front door.

Not nearly secure enough. How would he fix that? He turned to study their surroundings for an answer and caught her staring at him like he'd grown an extra head.

"Why would I think we're in danger?" She pointed to the hearth. "I was worried about the fire."

"Oh." *Whoops.*

"You don't honestly think we're in danger," she said, with a hint of incredulity to her voice.

He could let her live in her little fantasy world. Let her believe she was perfectly safe, but it wouldn't really serve her, would it? Better to know there was a threat out there, so she might actually protect herself. Lock doors. Be safe.

"What do you think happened back there when we crashed?"

Her frown deepened, but then she rubbed her head as it clearly hurt her wound. "I... You slid off the road into the ditch. Because of the weather."

He raised his eyebrows. "How did you hit your head?"

"That part is a little...fuzzy, but you slid into a ditch. Why wouldn't I hit my head?"

"Not that side of it. Not the way we fell. We were hit, Kate. By another car. Easy enough to do with the snow that bad, though a bit strange out here in the middle of nowhere. Still, I was willing to believe it was an accident. Until the other driver kept going, and rammed us again straight into that ditch."

"But... Why?"

He knew she was smart and capable, but he supposed

what she *was* was frightened and out of her depth. Everyone around her had convinced her that she was always just overreacting, though she had probably been right about her suspicions of being followed or watched when her father first disappeared.

Maybe someone had even wanted her to *believe* she was overreacting, to stop looking into things. There was a lot still to uncover—not just about her father's disappearance, but about those early months after.

"You said you thought someone was following you back when this all started."

She shook her head. "Brody. Honestly, you have to understand. I was bereft. I couldn't sleep. I kept bugging the police and… I wasn't myself. I wasn't in control."

"Maybe not, but that doesn't mean someone wasn't watching you as you poked and prodded at the case. And what happened when you let up? Or hid it better?"

She looked taken aback.

"You're trying to act like you let it go. But all that research wasn't done in the first few years. And you came to me. Maybe you dialed it back, maybe you kept it on the down low, but you've never stopped looking for your father. You were just doing it quietly. Then I came in and did it not so quietly."

She still didn't say anything. She stood there, looking like he'd punched her. He wanted to take it all back. Reach out and soothe her somehow. But Brody didn't know how to sugarcoat the truth. Not when she'd be in more danger if she didn't accept it.

"There is something about Stanley Music that someone doesn't want you to know, Kate. It's too much of a coincidence otherwise."

"But..." She clearly couldn't think of any way to refute that, though she wanted to. "I'm sorry, you want me to believe after ten years of everything I've done, you come along and in a few hours find the one thing that..." She trailed off, looking pained.

He went over to the first-aid kit and went through everything until he found some painkillers it would be safe for her to take with that concussion.

"Sometimes an investigation needs someone who knows nothing. You knew your father was a music teacher, so the invoices made sense to you. The police too. And probably any private investigator. They were looking for irregularities, and that wasn't one."

"So, why did it stick out to you?"

He handed her two of the pills and then a water bottle. She stared at both with some distrust. "Your head hurts. You'll feel better if you take them."

She heaved out a sigh, but took the pills and the water. She swallowed both down. She lowered herself into one of the rickety chairs at the kitchen table. "You're trying to avoid the question," she said after a few minutes of silence. "If the police were looking for irregularities, what was it that you were looking for that made this stand out to you—and you alone, after years of cops, investigators?"

"And years of your own research?"

"I never knew what I was looking for. I was just... searching."

"You should give yourself more credit. I can't think

of too many people who would have put together the kind of organized, comprehensive information you have. And it just might lead to answers, if we're careful. If you let me—"

"Stop avoiding the question," she snapped. "Why you?"

He didn't have to answer her. He didn't owe her any damn thing, but he *felt* like he did. Regardless of what his brain tried to tell him. "I was trained to look beyond the obvious, beyond what people want you to see. It's not like police work, where you go off the facts and the evidence. It's…more complicated than that."

"Trained," she echoed. She looked up at him with those soft brown eyes. "In the army?"

"Yeah." He had the strangest desire to tell her everything. Everything he'd been. Everything he'd done. It was impossible, but he *wanted* to, and he was more shaken by that need than he cared to admit.

"Why not threaten me back when I was sixteen? Why not crash my car or whatever when I was little more than a sad, desperate teenager?"

"Well, the timing might have made things all the more suspicious. By waiting, they take any heat off. Keep it separate." But they could have attacked Kate when she was alone. She seemed to be alone and isolated an awful lot. Instead, they'd stolen the invoices, presumably. Then waited until she was with someone else to try and cause some damage.

"You don't think that," Kate said flatly, as if she could see into the inner workings of his brain. "You think something else."

Brody sighed. "Your father might have left, but he's still your father. He might not have wanted you hurt."

"You think my father..."

"I just think there's a possibility the man who disappeared is involved in...whatever this is to try and cover up whatever Stanley Music is."

Chapter Nine

"I'm very tired," Kate said, because she was. Because the exhaustion burrowed so deep she wanted to cry. Not deal with any of this.

Her father. Alive. Stealing invoices? Warning her, but not hurting her? But not *not* hurting her, because her head throbbed. Her body just ached. Everything was off and wrong.

And this man standing there, looking at her with *pity* in his mesmerizing hazel eyes. It was all wrong. This was *not* her life.

"Take your boots and socks off and I'll try to dry them by the fire. Sleep for a bit. Probably not more than two hours. You seem pretty good for a concussion, but we can't be too careful."

We. That felt so very strange. But she nodded and got to her feet. She felt like dead weight and everything was far too complicated to sort through. Maybe if she went to sleep, she'd wake up and things would make any kind of sense.

She took her boots and socks off. They weren't too

bad, but having them nice and warm when she woke up would be nice.

She crawled into the bed—for all the living history she'd done here, she'd never actually crawled onto the bed with its straw mattress, grass-stuffed pillow and old scratchy blankets. Much as she loved history, she was rather a fan of modern comfort. But she was so tired she thought she could have slept in the middle of a snowbank.

Brody crouched down next to the bed, so that he was almost eye level with her.

"I'm not going anywhere," he said, making it sound like a grave promise. "I'm going to help you until you have answers."

She laughed, wondering idly if she was delirious. "Why?"

He studied her, then reached out. He gently smoothed the stray strand of hair that had fallen over her face and tucked it behind her ear. His fingertips just barely brushing the skin behind her ear. If she'd been standing, her legs would have given out.

"It's the right thing to do."

She wished he wouldn't have said that. It meant too much to her. Made all those jangled, scared feelings inside of her soften too much.

But then he stood and she closed her eyes, and it felt like not two minutes later she was being shaken.

"Come on, Kate. Wake up now."

She groaned. She wanted to roll over and pull the covers over her head, but he tugged them away instead.

"Sleepy," she muttered.

"I just bet. But you need to get up for a bit. I made coffee."

"Coffee." She managed to blink her eyes open. Brody was sitting on the bed, pushing her up into a sitting position next to him. She blinked blearily at the wood stove. "You made coffee on that?"

"I'm very resourceful. Practically a pioneer myself." He pulled her to her feet. "Kind of amazing what they managed to do with how little they had, isn't it?"

"That is exactly what is amazing." She had the same thought, day in and day out at work. She loved finding all the ways people had persevered with so very little. She loved trying to impart that knowledge to people.

Because humans had been surviving the unthinkable since the beginning of time, and finding ways to live and love throughout that darkest of it.

Brody hauled her to her feet. She wavered. Though her feet were steady underneath her, her vision twirled for a moment.

Brody held her by the elbows, keeping her upright. "You let me know when you're steady."

She stared at him. He'd woken her up because of the concussion. He was holding her up, waiting for her to be steady. There was a growth of dark whiskers—darker than his brown hair—all over his chin. He looked vaguely disreputable, but he was holding her like she were glass.

She reached out and touched his chin before she could think better of it. "Prickly."

His eyebrows raised, and his mouth curved, and somewhere in the back of her head she had the thought this was probably inappropriate. But she was too tired to work up any embarrassment.

"Coffee," she said. When he tried to help her over to the chair, she pulled one arm free and patted his shoulder with it. "I'm steady now."

He let her go, but she noticed he hovered right behind her as she made her way to the kitchen table. Once she was seated and he was certain she was steady, he went to the coffeepot.

He poured the coffee into one of the tin cups they kept in the cupboard. The coffee looked a little thick, and she much preferred cream and sugar, but they didn't have any of that. So, she'd have to choke it down black.

He set the cup in front of her, studying her. "How do you feel?"

"Like death," she replied, blowing on the coffee.

He chuckled. Then poured himself a cup.

"You probably want to sleep."

"No, I'm good." He sat in the chair across from her. The only light came from the fireplace and the lanterns she'd lit last night. But the cabin was now warm and cozy against the howling world outside.

It couldn't last. She might be tired—heck, she might be delirious—but she understood this was nothing but a respite from what came next. If Brody was right, and someone had crashed into them on purpose, she was in danger.

Danger.

It was hard to wrap her mind around, and yet… She looked at Brody, sipping his hot black coffee without even a wince. She had no doubt he'd know how to handle danger. And he seemed determined to help her. No matter how little she understood *that*, she believed it.

"So, what comes next, Brody?"

He didn't pretend to misunderstand her. He put his cup down, leaned his elbows on the table and considered. "Once it's morning, I think we should go back to your office. The invoices might be gone, but we still have the credit card statements. I'm going to have to find a way to look into Stanley Music that doesn't raise any suspicions. Once we can get out of here, I think… Kate, I don't think you should be alone until we know who hit us."

"But I'm always alone."

He frowned. "I thought you lived with your mother."

"Well, yes, but…"

"I understand if you don't want her to be in danger, but—"

"I can't decide if you're purposefully misunderstanding me or if it's just so incomprehensible to you, you can't wrap your head around it. Didn't you say yourself your mother was no prize?"

"Yes, I said that."

"Then you should understand that we are not…that way. My mother and I might live together, but in separate wings. She doesn't like me. She doesn't spend time with me. We exist…in parallel universes. She does what she wants—I take care of everything as long as it's carefully out of sight."

"That's pretty cruel, Kate."

"She would agree with you."

He frowned even deeper. "I meant her. *She* is pretty

cruel. At least my mom just took off whenever she didn't want to be around. I certainly didn't have to look after her."

Somehow, despite the fact that he was this big strong ex-soldier of a man who'd carried her through a blizzard, and promised to help her figure this out because it was the right thing to do, it was far too easy to picture him as a little boy without a mother.

"I don't know why we're talking about this." She rubbed at her temple, under the bandage. "I'm not myself."

"Seems to me you're being exactly yourself, instead of hiding it all under some biddable exterior, but that's not you."

She laughed. Bitterly. "Oh, yeah, how?"

"If you were biddable, you'd have friends. You'd have a framework. An ecosystem." He waved the room around them. "But you have this job you love, and you've made some kind of manageable life for yourself in the wreckage of what had to be pretty devastating."

SHE STARED AT HIM, and Brody didn't really know what she saw. He wished he could…make this easier on her. But the only way out was through. This might be *her* problem, but he had a feeling something he'd done had kicked off the renewed interest in her. Snowmobiles and car accidents.

Part of her being some sort of target was his fault, and he'd see this through to the end. Make sure she was safe.

"Maybe I should be a little more biddable so I'd have an *ecosystem*," she said at length. "Who says ecosystem?"

"Someone who's made a study out of people and groups and how they work." Brody tried not to bristle. She had a head injury and had been thrust into something she didn't—couldn't—understand. "I know you're overwhelmed." He stilled her tapping hand by putting his own over hers on the table. He tried to ignore the stab of gratification that she stilled at his touch. "This is a lot. But we'll figure it out. I promise you that."

"If..." She swallowed, and she didn't tug her hand away. She let it lay there, under his. Small, but not fragile. She met his gaze. "If my father stole those invoices, he's here. Close. If he's hiding something bigger than disappearing..." She closed her eyes. "I just wanted to find him. To have closure. To understand what he'd really done—to Amberleigh, to anyone else. That's all I wanted. Instead I'm opening up a can of worms."

"Maybe. But there might be closure in that can of worms."

"I feel like I'm sixteen again. Losing *everything* I thought I knew. Alone."

Brody squeezed her hand. "But you're not alone. Not this time."

She shook her head, opened her eyes and fixed him with a heartbreaking look. "Why?"

"You asked for my help."

"That doesn't guarantee someone is going to help, Brody. I definitely learned that lesson."

"It does when you ask me. Besides, I like you, Kate. You might not see it in yourself, but I see someone who built the life they wanted and that suited them with what little they were given. Kind of like those pioneers you like so much."

After a moment of stunned silence, she pulled her hand out from under his. He had to resist the urge to hold fast, and he wasn't at all comfortable with that urge, so he folded his hands behind his head.

"I'm starting to believe you're too good to be true," she said, studying him suspiciously. "What secret are you hiding? Do you keep corpses in your attic? Kill animals? Have bird pets?"

"What's wrong with bird pets?"

"I don't know. They're creepy."

"I have none of those things." But he did have a secret, one he hadn't been so adept at hiding. He'd figured back when they'd been sent here that it'd be easy to pretend to be someone he wasn't. Hadn't he made a career out of that?

But it was different when it wasn't a mission. When it was just life—even if it wasn't your own. He was still himself, even if himself was this Brody Thompson, rookie rancher. But he wasn't playing a role, or trying to keep his country safe.

"I know it's not morning, but you grabbed some flashlights, right?"

"Yes." And he needed to focus on this little mission he'd made for himself, rather than…anything to do with his past.

"Then let's go over to the office building. Get the files now. What's the point of sitting here, sipping coffee, feeling sorry for me?"

"Not a good idea. We don't know who's out there.

Going out in the dark with flashlights is like a shining beacon of *please kill me*."

"You can't really believe..." She trailed off. "Someone really...purposefully crashed us into a ditch?"

Brody nodded. "I'm sure of it."

"But they didn't kill us."

"No. Though leaving us crashed in the middle of a blizzard wasn't exactly a kindness. Who would have thought I'd have the skills to get us to safety?"

"Carry me to safety," she muttered. "Certainly not me." She sighed. "Then what are we supposed to do all night? Sit here and knit?"

He opened his mouth to say something—something he absolutely should *not* say, or think, or allow his brain to even form words for. He pushed it aside. "I think I'll take a little nap, if that's okay with you?"

She studied him quizzically, but she nodded. So he got up and went to the strange pioneer bed. It'd be good to rest while they had nothing to do. Come morning there'd be plenty, and clearly he needed a little more mental clarity.

He situated himself on the rickety bed, half feeling like his large frame would break it. Worse, the pillow smelled like her. Something vaguely flowery the snow and head wound should have dulled before she laid down.

But he closed his eyes, used all his old army tricks for falling asleep even in stressful or uncomfortable conditions and was out within seconds.

When he woke up, Kate was quietly moving around the stove. It looked and smelled like she was putting together some kind of breakfast. Though the fire and lanterns were giving off most of the light, he could tell that even if it was still dark outside, it was starting to brighten.

He sat up, and though Kate didn't look over her shoulder at him, she had to have heard him move.

"You talk in your sleep," she said, her tone carefully devoid of any kind of inflection that might give him a clue to what kind of things he talked about. In his sleep.

He sat on the bed, scratching a hand through his hair. "Oh, yeah? About what?"

"I couldn't understand all of it," she said carefully. She turned, put a plate of food on the table and gestured him for it. "But you mentioned Cal *a lot*."

Brody winced as he walked over to the table. His stomach rumbled. "That is a look into my psyche I could do without," he grumbled. "Are those homemade biscuits?"

"I had all night. I could only entertain myself reading for so long." She gestured to a book on the table. It was a diary of some kind. "I've read it a million times. Practically memorized it. So I figured cooking would be the next best thing."

He flipped open the cover. "Good reading?"

"For some. It's the journal of the first owner of this cabin. Well, a photocopied replica. We have to keep the original in better archival conditions. But the writer was Sarah Marks. I show it on some of the tours or read little parts to give them an idea of what the day-to-day was like."

"And what was it like?"

"Hard," she said with a laugh. "Lonely," she added, a little more seriously. "Sarah had a rough life. She left everything she knew back east, then lost her husband, her baby."

"Sounds depressing."

"I suppose. More melancholy than depressing." She took her own plate and sat across from him. "There's something comforting about… Well, it's hard to feel sorry for yourself too much when you know struggles are just part of it."

"Part of what?"

"Life."

He couldn't argue with that. "This is amazing, Kate."

"You're just hungry."

"The cookies were amazing, too."

She looked down at her plate, but she couldn't quite hide the smile of pleasure. "I like to cook," she said simply. "I had a look outside. I'm not sure we're getting out of here today."

"That bad?"

"I can't remember this much snow. Not in the past few years. And likely even if your brothers could get out here, they've got their hands full dealing with the cattle."

"I suppose as long as we can hike over to the office building and do some research, all's not lost. Maybe the weather will keep anyone after you at a distance."

But they'd definitely be taking some precautions before they walked over.

Chapter Ten

It was kind of nice to eat breakfast with someone. And Brody didn't force the conversation to stick to her father and the missing invoices. He asked about Sarah and the cabin, like he had an interest.

She knew better than to go into one of her long involved lectures only she and maybe Mr. Field and Hazeleigh cared about, but he asked good questions. Interested questions. It gave her warm fuzzy feelings—ones she should put a stop to.

They cleaned up breakfast, Brody standing hip to hip with her as they used boiled snow to wash everything. She fumbled things a few times, but didn't dare look at him to see his reaction.

He was being nice. He had some sort of misguided superhero complex. Save the little lady. And she needed the help, so she'd take it. And not get any ideas. If he *liked* her as he claimed, it was the friendly sort of like. Probably thought of her as some kid sister.

"How old are you?" she asked before she could think better of it.

She didn't dare look at his expression, and his voice

didn't give anything away as he answered her. "Thirty. How old are you?"

"Twenty-six."

"Not so far off."

That response shocked her enough to look up at him, and he was looking down at her and… She darted away, putting the dried plates and cooking utensils back where they belonged, creating some much needed distance.

"Sun should be up well enough now," she said brightly.

He agreed and they piled on all the layers they had, even fashioning blankets to act as scarves. Brody emptied out her backpack carefully, then strapped it on in case they needed to bring back any more supplies.

She opened the door and winced at both the brightness—even of dawn's light—and the cold wind.

"I don't suppose you know how to shoot a gun," he asked conversationally.

"Sure I do. You know, presuming it's a nineteenth-century era gun."

Brody laughed, which made her frown.

"What on earth are you laughing at?"

"Sorry, I just had a very clear image of you in your pioneer garb, skirts blowing in the wind, pointing one of those rifles at some dirty lowlife. Like an old Western."

"And that's funny?"

"It's far too appealing, Kate."

Which shut her up, because what was she supposed to say to that? Appealing? Who thought *any* of that was appealing?

"I don't suppose you've got any weapons lying around?" he asked.

"Up at the main building. Locked up, of course. You don't really think we'll need..." She trailed off when she saw his gun. From *this* century. "Oh."

"Just a precaution."

"Of course."

"Make you nervous?"

"Not the gun so much as the reason you're holding it." She looked around at the bright, blinding white world. Was someone really out there, wanting them dead? He had to be overthinking.

"I want you to stay put—just for a minute, while I take a quick look around."

"Brody..."

"Just a precaution. You can leave the door open, just don't step out yet. I'm going to walk around the cabin, look for tracks, signs of anyone."

"Okay," she agreed, reluctantly. He nodded, then stepped out into the cold morning. The snow reached his knees, and she watched him as he disappeared around the corner of the cabin. The gun in his hand looking both menacing and like it belonged there.

She heaved out a breath, watched the fog of it swirl and then disappear. She squinted out over to the main fort building, and then the office buildings. It was a short walk, though it'd take longer in the snow.

It struck her, in these random quiet moments, how insane this was. Surely her father wasn't stealing bits of her research. Surely no one was trying to get them killed. And surely Brody Thompson—former soldier, current rancher, too hot for anyone's own good—wasn't helping her and saying things about liking her, finding her *appealing.*

She'd had a psychotic break.

But after a few minutes, Brody reappeared. Still holding that gun. Still far too attractive bundled to the hilt. "Looks to be clear. Let's go."

"You didn't see anything?" she asked, stepping forward into the white. She tested the snow, hoping for a hard pack, but her foot sank up to the thigh.

"No sign of anyone. Which was about what I figured. The blizzard was too much. Whoever hit us had to have retreated back to wherever they have shelter."

When Kate struggled to pull her leg out of the snow to make the next step, Brody chuckled.

"I could carry you again," he offered.

"I can do it," Kate muttered. And she did, but it was slow going. She had to hold onto Brody's arm at times, to leverage herself up and out of the practically waist-deep snow.

But they got to the office building, and she fished her keys out of her coat pocket and opened the door. They stepped into the dark building. She flipped a switch and nothing happened. "Electricity is still down, which means no internet."

"Damn," he muttered. "Until we can get more information about Stanley Music, we're kind of at a stalemate."

Kate blew out a breath. "Maybe I've got something about them in the paperwork that we just missed the first time around." She doubted it, but she headed for her office anyway. She'd spent ten years on compiling all her records. Maybe she didn't remember everything, but she'd have remembered that or looked twice at it. "Or maybe it used to be a business and we have some record of it..." They didn't keep Wilde records in the fort that weren't directly *related* to the fort, but she had access to digitized records and...

Her thoughts stumbled to a stop as she looked at her office. It wasn't messy exactly, but she could just tell it wasn't as she'd left it.

You were mad at Brody. You weren't paying attention. Don't go down this paranoid road again.

It was her mother's voice in her head, and it was right of course. She'd had a concussion at this point. She wasn't thinking clearly. Brody wasn't helping with his stories of being run off the road or...

"What is it?"

Kate inhaled sharply, because she hadn't been breathing. She'd been spiraling. She hated that feeling. *Hated* it.

"I just left in such a rush. Didn't realize what a mess I'd left." She tried to think. Really think. Past the car accident. Past all the ideas Brody had *put* into her head.

Brody laid his hand on her shoulder. A gentle, but anchoring pressure. "Kate."

She looked up at him, and she wanted to be able to tell him that everything was fine. As it should be. But he looked...concerned, and all those times her mother had told her she was losing her mind, convinced her she was paranoid, it wasn't concern.

Kate had tried to convince herself it was. Mixed up in grief and betrayal that she'd taken out on Kate through no fault of her own.

But Brody was showing more care than her mother… ever had. It had always been Dad who was the compassionate one. Any warmth or happiness in her childhood had come from him, and then he left.

"Stuff's been moved around," Kate said, very quietly. Very carefully. If Brody told her she was making things up, she might just crumple.

But he held her gaze, very serious. "What exactly?"

"I don't know. Little things. My chair should be pushed into my desk. My computer monitor isn't usually pulled forward like that. Maybe Mr. Field…" But she trailed off. Because, of course, Mr. Field hadn't been in. No one had been in. There'd been a blizzard.

"Come with me." He didn't give her the opportunity to agree or disagree. He was already pulling her along, back to the front door. He released her and swung the door open.

He studied the door, front and back. Crouched, practically got nose to nose with the knob. "Someone broke in," Brody confirmed. "But took great pains to make it look like they hadn't."

Kate lowered herself into a chair. This couldn't be… But why would Brody lie? Why would he be trying to confirm all her worst thoughts? Unless they were true.

Unless they were always true.

"I wasn't paranoid. I wasn't unhinged. This whole time. This *whole* time, someone has been paying attention to me." Kate let her face fall into her hands. Her body ached, her head throbbed, but the idea that she had never been wrong, never been off base…

It wasn't closure, but for the first time in ten years she felt…lighter. Surer.

She'd been right. All along.

"It couldn't have been about Amberleigh, or at least just about her. We know he didn't kill her, that somewhere along the line they parted ways—*if* they left together. He's not covering up a murder, but he—or someone—is trying to hide *something*. And have been, for ten years."

Ten years. She wished she could race home and tell her mother right now.

I was right. I was right all along.

She wanted to laugh, but that wasn't what bubbled up inside of her. It was much closer to a sob, and her eyes filled and… *Oh, hell.*

Anguish just poured out of her. She couldn't stop it. Ten years of the mental gymnastics of talking herself out of things, and to know she had been right. Maybe there were still things she didn't know, but at the heart of it she hadn't been clinging to a fantasy.

"Hey, hey. It's all right. It'll be all right. We'll get it all figured out. Don't cry." Brody patted her shoulder awkwardly, which *did* make her laugh. She wiped her face and tried to find some control.

"It's not a…worried, sad cry, exactly." She inhaled deeply and let it out. "Just ten years' worth of relief."

"You were right."

She looked up at him and managed a smile, though she knew her face must be a mess. "I was right. When everyone convinced me I was wrong. It doesn't untangle everything that's been tangled, but some things,

I guess. It's like a relief. After all this time. Part of a weight lifted off my shoulders." But there was still a weight there. "You think it was my father."

"I think it has to involve your father in some way. Someone has kept their eye on you, without harming you in any way—at least until I got involved."

"Or Stanley Music got involved."

Brody nodded. "Fair point. We need to figure out that piece of the puzzle, but I guess the world is currently against us in that respect."

"It's waited ten years. I suppose it can wait another few days."

"Look, it's up to you, but Landon's got a way with computers. If they haven't lost power, if they've got time to spare beyond the cattle, I can ask him to look into it while we're stuck here."

Kate bit her lip. "Will that make him some kind of target?"

"He'll be able to keep it on the down low. Better than I would. I would have asked him in the first place if I'd thought digging into it would unearth anything other than…well, old information."

"I can't imagine they have power, but if you think he can help, that's fine."

Brody nodded, pulled his phone out of his pocket. "I don't have much battery left. What about you?"

Kate pulled her phone out of her pocket. "Plenty. You want to use mine?"

"Yeah, thanks." He took her phone and called his brother.

While Kate stared at the door, wondering what happened now that she was right.

"CAL WON'T LIKE IT."

Brody scowled into the phone. "What does Cal like these days?"

Landon chuckled. "Fair enough. I'll see what I can do once the power's back. Zara's putting us through the paces with all this special blizzard cattle care. I won't be back at the house for another couple hours. And I can't imagine coming to get you guys today. Roads are toast, and you've got our best vehicle."

Brody winced at that, but he didn't let on that the best vehicle was currently *toast.* "We can survive another day or two out here. I'd just like to get somewhere a little more..." Brody looked out the window. They were sitting ducks. Whoever had hit them was somewhere out there, and maybe they'd retreated thanks to the blizzard, but that wouldn't keep them away forever. Especially knowing those snowmobile tracks outside Kate's office yesterday were probably theirs. "Well, I'd like Kate to have a doctor check her out. She's got a nasty bump."

"We'll get someone out to you by tomorrow, for sure," Landon said. "Even if we have to call some kind of emergency services. But you know how to look after a bump."

"Yeah, I do."

"Enjoy ringing in the New Year stuck in 1895," Landon said with a laugh.

"*The New Year...*" Brody echoed.

"Yeah, have you lost track of time? Today's December thirty-first. See you next year, bro," Landon offered. "We'll check in again tomorrow, see where we're at."

"Yeah. Tomorrow. Later." He pressed End on the phone, then turned to Kate. She was pale, the bandage on her head probably needing redressing. Her eyes were red from her crying jag, and he couldn't imagine what it would be like to just…carry all that grief and anxiety around for ten years.

And she'd never given up. Even when she'd clearly told herself she had. It was kind of a miracle. He'd lost that kind of faith in just about everything. Except his brothers.

"Well, I guess we're spending New Year's Eve together, Kate."

She laughed. Which he didn't quite understand, but she looked genuinely amused by the notion.

"Missing out on a big party?"

"Oh, yes, that's me. Big party plans on New Year's Eve. It's never just me alone, watching the ball drop and eating an entire cake by myself."

"Alone? Really?"

"I'd get a cat, but I'm allergic."

"Kate…"

"Have I given the impression I have friends? Hazeleigh is the closest thing I've got and that's complicated. Certainly too complicated for New Year midnight countdowns." But she didn't sound like she was complaining, or that she felt lonely. "What about you? Big New Year's traditions?"

Traditions? Most of his adult life had been spent deployed or in army barracks. He'd never had much reason to take leave. That's why he'd become part of Team Breaker. "I can't remember the last New Year's Eve I wasn't with my brothers. That's about it."

"I always wanted a sibling. Like the Harts. They always had each other." For the first time she sounded wistful.

It made his chest hurt. All the ways she was alone that mirrored in a lot of ways his own…isolation growing up. Much like her, he'd found a purpose in his profession. But he'd also found a family.

"I don't suppose you've got any champagne around here, then?"

Her mouth curved, some of that wistfulness leaving her face. "I very much doubt it, but we can raid the kitchen and see what we can come up with." She sighed. "What were they doing in my stuff, Brody?"

"I don't know, but I'd say you still have—or had—something someone wanted. We could go through and see if you notice anything else missing?"

She sighed heavily, but got to her feet and nodded. They went back to her office and she surveyed everything with a critical eye. She sat at her desk chair, rifled through the folders. "Something is missing," she muttered to herself.

Brody let her work and studied the office from a stranger's eye. It'd be easy to pick out the things that didn't connect to her work at the fort. She kept everything organized and labeled. But why now?

He truly believed something he'd done to look into Stanley Music had prompted whoever was out there to make a move, but either she had something about

Stanley Music in there they hadn't seen, or there was something else as well.

"I looked into the other invoices, music stores and the like, right? But maybe we need to focus on anything relating to music."

"Okay."

She handed him a couple folders and he began looking through with a critical eye. Anything relating to music he set to the side. They worked in silence for a while.

"That's what's missing," she said suddenly. "I had an appointment book in here of Dad's that had lists of all the lessons—dates, people, how much they owed and if they paid."

Brody leaned against the doorframe and considered this new information. "They don't know exactly what they're looking for or they would have got it the first time."

She chewed on her bottom lip as she surveyed the little piles they'd made in the cramped room. "So, it's probably not my dad. And they might be back."

"Both possibilities." And it all connected to lessons and music. "Something wasn't on the up and up with your dad's music lessons."

She looked up at him. "He did teach music, though. I learned to play the violin and so did Amberleigh—even if something else was going on, there was something legitimate there."

"Makes it a better cover."

"For what?"

Brody considered. "I don't know how much you

heard about Amberleigh's murder, but she was involved with a group that ran and sold drugs. That doctor might have killed her, but it was all because she was messed up in this group involved in drug running."

"But wasn't the group all arrested after shooting Jake?"

"Supposedly. But all it takes is one of the higher-ups not getting caught, or even more likely, it's a system of groups."

"An *eco*system?"

He glared at her, but it was hard to hold when she was smiling at him. Teasing him. "Something like that," he returned. "Let's get all the music stuff together. We'll take it with us, but leave this looking the way it was so if they do try to come back, they might not notice that we've taken some things."

They worked for another few hours, separating and compiling. Brody turned over the question of *why now* in his head, and at the end of the day, he had to believe whoever was doing this hadn't been aware of just how much information Kate had. Until looking into Stanley Music had tipped them off.

Once they'd gotten through everything, and put what they didn't need away, Brody glanced at his watch. "We should head back to the cabin. We'll be losing daylight soon. Let's go raid that kitchen."

She nodded and they put the layers of clothing they'd taken off back on. When they stepped outside, the sky was a deep, vibrant pink. The clouds were lighter shades, giving dimension and little wisps of fiery gold.

The mountains seemed to absorb that gold and practically throb with the color of it.

Kate breathed out and stopped for a moment, and Brody found himself stopping, too. Transfixed by the beautiful sunset.

"This is why they stayed," she said, and he had a feeling she was talking more to herself than purposefully trying to tell him anything. But he listened all the same. "Hard day, terrible blizzard. You're tired, you're hungry, but you came this far, and at the end of the day, you see something like this to remind you that you came here for a reason."

There was a truth to her words that echoed inside him, but only for a moment before he remembered they were targets. Anyone could be out there, lurking in this beautiful world of hers. "How'd they celebrate the New Year on the frontier?" he asked, pulling her forward so they could get moving.

"Not much differently than any other day," she said, gripping his arm to help her leverage her legs over and through the snow. "It was hard to get anything special out here, or visit with neighbors. Most efforts had just been done for Christmas, and with the winter weather, travel was less likely. They'd have chores at the crack of dawn, so staying up till midnight wasn't very popular. Different traditions might have been brought depending on where you came from, but for Sarah Marks it was just another day, mostly."

Just another day. He could certainly relate to that. But it seemed wrong to treat it that way when Kate didn't go to parties, or have friends, didn't even have a mother who cared enough about her welfare to spend time with her. She was alone.

He knew from experience that even when it was more comfortable to be alone, it wasn't always the easiest thing. She pulled her keys out and pushed them into the lock. She twisted, and then she stilled.

"Brody." She looked up at him, holding her keys in the door, not pushing it open. Her eyes were wide, concerned. "It wasn't locked."

Chapter Eleven

Brody's expression changed completely. Right before her eyes. Yet it didn't seem like he moved a muscle. But everything got harder. His eyes narrowed, and his hand very carefully moved through the air to close over hers on the keys.

His other hand held the gun.

Nerves jittered up Kate's spine, but she breathed through them. Whatever was going on, she could be brave. She could be like Brody. Stoic and certain.

"I don't see any tracks, do you?"

They both surveyed the snow around them, but though the wind wasn't whipping around like yesterday, it was certainly still blowing the snow into drifts and peaks that would obscure footprints. Even as she looked back at their own just walking over from the office buildings, they'd been obscured. Visible indentations, but harder to determine how many people, what size.

"I don't see anything."

Brody frowned, staring at something around the corner. "Don't move, okay?"

She nodded and he took his hand off hers. He moved

carefully over to the cabin, peered around, then immediately pulled his head back. He stalked back to her, grim and blank.

"Go to the cabin," he said, his voice barely above a whisper. "Quick as you can. Lock whatever you can, barricade the rest."

"But you—"

"Have a gun and fighting experience. You don't, Kate. If someone is in there, I will be able to handle it. If no one is in there, I'll come get you."

Kate struggled with the order. After all, Brody was only here because of her. But he *did* have experience she didn't have. Fighting and guns. He'd been a soldier. He knew how to deal with a threat.

"What did you see?"

"Not sure, but it could be snowmobile tracks. Go to the cabin."

Kate looked across the long yard to the cabin. Where it had felt safe. And warm. She did want to go there, but not without him. She turned to face him. "Be honest with me, isn't alone more dangerous than together?"

"No. I promise, if anything is in there, it's a threat I can handle. But only if I don't have to worry about you."

Kate inhaled. She wanted to listen, because going to the cabin sounded much safer than trailing after him. But what if he got hurt? That scrape on his back was bad enough, if he went in there alone—

He put his hand over hers again, pulled the keys out carefully. He moved her fingers so she curled them around the keychain. He squeezed. "Now, Kate."

She could argue. Say she could hold her own. She

could listen to her conscience and not let him handle this alone, but all of those were dumb choices. It put both of them in danger, and had more to do with her wanting to be seen as brave when she wasn't than with common sense.

She had to trust him. "Just be careful. Don't take any unnecessary chances. We just want to be safe. You don't need to be a superhero."

Something in his expression changed—she couldn't read it, but there was something softer in it. "Go on. Fast as you can. I'm not going in till you're safe inside."

She nodded and started out. The high snowdrifts made running impossible, but she moved as quickly as her body and the snow would allow. She told herself the whole way that this was *precaution*. Brody would open the main building, and maybe someone had been in there, but they'd have to be long gone by now.

They would have heard a snowmobile. In the office building, for sure, they would have heard the engine puttering up to the main building. Maybe if it had come last night in the blizzard when they'd been hunkered down at the cabin they wouldn't have heard it, but this morning?

There was no way anyone had snuck up on them. No way anyone was in that building.

And there's no way someone came out here last night in the middle of that storm?

She looked back at Brody. He was still waiting by the door. His hand was on the knob, and he held the gun in his other hand. As much as that gun was a sign of all the bad things, he looked completely right somehow, standing in the middle of all that white, his hand clasped around his weapon.

He'd been a soldier. She reminded herself of that over and over again as she returned her focus to the cabin. He'd been a soldier, and knew how to fight. He had all those scars, and yet he was all in one piece.

Because he knew what he was doing. This wasn't just about protecting her. It was about protecting them. Finding the truth. She'd asked for his help, and in Brody's mind that meant…helping until the problem was solved.

She didn't know men like that. She hadn't believed they existed. Not since her dad had left her and shattered any illusion she had about… Well, everything.

She finally made it to the front door, panting heavily but here. She unlocked the door. She gave Brody one last look. He was just a figure now at this distance. She couldn't make out his expression, only the shape of him.

She swallowed down the anxiety, the fear. For the first time, she fully put her trust in someone and prayed it wouldn't come back to bite her in the butt.

She stepped inside the cabin. Brody had told her to lock and barricade everything, but she wanted to leave the door open for the time being. If Brody came, she wanted him to be able to get in quickly. So, she started at the back. There were only windows to worry about here, but they were low enough to the ground and big enough to be entrance points if someone broke the glass.

She couldn't exactly board them up. It would ruin the historical integrity of the cabin and—

Are you really standing here worried about histor-

ical integrity under the current, potentially dire circumstances?

Okay, well, even if she had the supplies to board up the windows, it would take too long. She surveyed the room. If she put the table on its side, it would cover most of the window. It wasn't very heavy, but if she reinforced it with some heavier items, it would definitely be difficult to get through.

She set about doing all of that, trying not to fret about Brody. Just focus on the tasks. That was how she'd gotten through a lot of her life.

She got the windows mostly covered, or at least as good as it was going to get. For the front door, she could drag the stove over, maybe. It would be hard, and she wouldn't want to put it in front of the door quite yet. She'd wait for Brody. But she could get it closer.

She turned to study the stove and determine how hard it would be to move on her own. Then screamed when a man stepped out from the corner between the wall and stove—a gun in each hand.

"Don't move," he said. She didn't recognize him. Nothing about the weather-beaten face covered in black-and-gray whiskers and long hair was familiar to her.

But that voice. She knew that voice almost as well as she knew her own. "Dad?"

He pushed the hat he was wearing back enough so she could see his eyes. The dark brown of her own. Eyes she'd spent her entire childhood looking into.

She couldn't seem to breathe and tears filled her eyes. It was all wrong. He couldn't be here, holding guns, and yet… It was her dad. He was here. Ten years and she was standing in the same room as her father.

"Kate, you have to stop this."

"Stop…what?" Crying? A few tears had slipped down her cheeks, but that didn't seem fair. She hadn't seen him in ten years. And he was standing so far away, still holding those guns even if he was pointing them at the ground.

"All of it. The investigating. That friend of yours poking into things. I've kept you safe all this time, but I won't be able to if you keep this up. They'll kill you. They'll kill him. If he comes after us, he'll beg for death."

They and *us*. Kate couldn't make sense of it. Of any of it. "You disappeared without a word. Without a trace."

"Yes, and I thought that would solve everything. But you didn't let it go. So, this was the last resort. You have to stop, Kate. This is your last chance. Your only warning."

"Dad, you're here." *Here*. Her father was *here*. She could reach out and touch him. Hug him. But he held two guns and she didn't dare. It wasn't even out of fear exactly. She could just feel this…wall between them. Ten years and tons of secrets.

"You let this go, Kate. You don't tell *anyone* you saw me—not even your friend out there. Do you understand me?"

"No. I don't understand *any* of this."

"I have to go. I'm sorry. I am." He moved for the door, so quickly she reached out to stop him, but he'd already left the cabin.

She scurried after him. "Dad."

He walked with long purposeful strides in the opposite direction of the main building. “Dad!”

But he didn’t look back.

She took two steps and then stopped herself. He didn’t want her to follow. He didn’t want *her*.

He just wanted her to stop.

BRODY DIDN’T HEAR the scream, the shouts. He was already in the main building. It was silent as a tomb, what with the electricity out. But someone had jimmied the lock. Maybe they’d already left, but Brody had to be sure.

The building didn’t have the best lighting, so despite the bright sun bouncing off the white snow outside, the interior was dim.

He did his first sweep of the main room, studying the array of mannequins. They were particularly creepy in the heavy silence, alone. Faceless. Brody repressed a shudder. It was hard to notice if anything was different. He didn’t know the room well enough to notice subtle differences, and at the end of the day he didn’t know what these people were looking for if they’d already been through Kate’s office and papers—and more than once.

Still, he looked, determined not to leave any stone uncovered. He poked into closets, corners, behind exhibits. He was glad he’d been through the compound last night so he had a basic idea of the lay of the land. But he didn’t really know what would be off or wrong.

Maybe he should have kept Kate with him. He shook

his head. Sending her off to the cabin where she'd be safe. Protected.

Unless…

The cold grip of fear was no stranger. Brody had dealt with that every moment of his deployed years. Even more so when they'd been Team Breaker, and one mistake could have cost any of his brothers their lives.

But fear could cost as many lives as it could save. He'd watched Kate walk to safety, and if they wanted her, they would have stuck around after the car accident. They would have taken or threatened her in the ten years she'd been living this—whatever it was.

The smart thing was the thing he'd chosen to do. He knew that in his gut. Even as he worried for Kate.

When you let yourself care, worry was a natural response to danger. Somehow…he'd allowed himself to care for Kate.

He snorted quietly. *Allowed* himself. It had hit him out of nowhere. Maybe that first moment he'd met her, giving a prim lecture in her pioneer costume. And everything he'd learned about her since didn't help that initial glimmer of interest. Attraction.

He'd always had great timing, hadn't he?

Grimly, Brody moved forward into the back of the building. The kitchenette and some changing rooms were here, and a back exit. Presumably, they'd chosen to break in to the front exit only, but they might have left through the back.

He poked his head into the changing rooms, then stilled. The hairs on the back of his neck stood up and he stopped breathing—focusing all his energy on listening.

He'd heard something. A very, very faint something—could have been a mouse, the wind—but it was *something* enough to be on extra alert.

He moved through the two changing rooms, making absolutely no noise. He kept his gun gripped at the ready, his breathing even, and his ears and eyes alert to every possible nuance around him.

He heard it again. The creak of a floorboard, not loud—muffled almost. But definitely made by something heavier than a mouse.

He moved toward it. The kitchenette was a small, cramped room—Brody knew that from yesterday. It was also the room that housed the back exit door. He edged toward the opening that would allow him to see into the room. He paused after every step, careful to be noiseless. Careful to have his gun ready and his instincts sharp.

He angled his body just so he could see a sliver of the room. The sliver with the door. It was closed. He didn't see anyone. So he inched forward.

Someone was in the room, shoving something into a backpack. Carefully, Brody raised his gun.

"Don't move," Brody ordered, holding his gun pointed directly at the man's back.

But the man whirled on Brody, his own gun out and pointed, pulling the trigger during the whirl.

Brody had to dive back behind the refrigerator as some kind of shield. The man kept shooting and Brody huddled there, inwardly cursing. He hadn't wanted to shoot first, but he could have debilitated the guy before saying anything. Maybe his instincts were getting rusty.

Not going to fly.

Brody crouched and waited for the man to appear so he could take him down, but he never did. Eventually, the gunshots stopped but still the man didn't come at him. Carefully, Brody eased his head out to survey where the gunman was, but there was nothing.

The door hung open.

He'd…run. Brody moved for the door, still careful and alert to make sure it wasn't some kind of trick or trap. But when he looked out the backdoor, there the shooter was. Zooming off into the blinding white on a snowmobile. Brody had no hope of catching up. The engine roared through the air—and another vehicle seemed to come out of nowhere to meet up with the first. In a few more seconds, they were gone and the world was quiet again.

Brody sighed. They were gone—more intent on escaping than on hurting him, which he supposed was a positive all in all. He'd need to get Kate up here to see if they'd taken anything.

Kate.

He practically vaulted back to the front of the building, whipped the door open. Took a few steps out into the snow to see the cabin.

And she was standing outside of it.

Chapter Twelve

Dad had disappeared. She'd stood there, sure he'd come back. Sure something would happen. But he'd disappeared into the vast world around them and…

She jumped about a foot when a loud *bang* pierced the air. "Oh, God." Her vision whipped to the main building. Brody… Dad had said…

If he comes after us, he'll beg for death.

"No, no, no." They couldn't.

Bang. Bang.

If they hurt Brody… She had to… Something.

She squeezed her eyes shut. *Stop panicking. Think.*

She couldn't go running in there. She didn't have a weapon. She didn't have anything. She had her phone. She would call for help. Maybe the roads were bad, but if people were *shooting,* someone would have to come *help.*

She fumbled in her coat pocket for the phone, her hands shaking as she drew it out, but before she could dial anything she heard a different sound. Like a door slamming, opening. She looked up and across to the main fort.

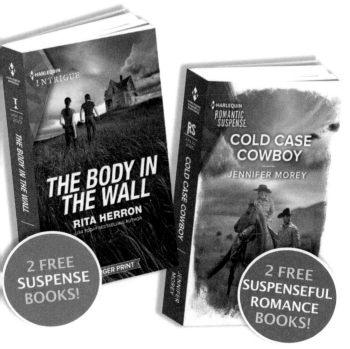

There was Brody. She couldn't make out his expression across the vast yard between them, but he immediately began to move for her. He didn't appear to be hurt.

Thank God. She ran for him as he stormed toward her, and when they met, she couldn't help but throw her arms around him. He was okay. In one piece. No visions of him bloody in the middle of her mannequins had come true. "I heard gunshots. I thought..."

He pulled her away from him, holding her by the elbows. "You should have stayed put. You should have stayed damn put."

There was a fury in his voice, in his eyes, but his hands were gentle, and she had the distinct impression he wanted to physically shake some sense into her. But he didn't.

"I heard *gunshots*."

He sighed. "None of them mine," he muttered, scanning the world around them. He was all *soldier* in that moment. Remote. Capable. "Let's get inside."

He let go of one of her arms, but not the other. There were enough tracks now that she didn't need as much help through the snow, but still he didn't let her go. They walked back into the cabin.

It had grown cold again, so many hours without a fire. Her pants were wet. Her heart was jittering in a million different ways.

She'd seen her father. She desperately wanted to tell Brody, but Dad had warned her not to. For his own good.

"I have no idea what's going on," Brody said, moving toward the fireplace. To her surprise, he set to restarting the fire with practiced ease. "You'll need to look around the main building to see what they took. The gunman had a backpack of some kind. He put something into it."

Brody stood, frowned. "He wasn't here alone. Two men on snowmobiles."

Had one been her father? Should she tell Brody… She looked up at him. He was so strong and sure and he'd been in the military. Maybe he could handle whatever her dad was mixed up in.

But she thought about the guns Dad had held. The things he'd said.

They'll kill you. They'll kill him. If he comes after us, he'll beg for death.

It had been her father. Alive. Here. Protecting her, so he said. She swallowed. She couldn't put Brody in the middle. This wasn't his family. His fight. He could get hurt or worse if he helped her and she had to…

She had to protect Brody.

The emotions swirling around inside of her were too much, but she had to control them. Swallow them down. She couldn't tell Brody she'd seen her father. She had to somehow…get out of all of this.

"I don't suppose there's anything we can do about it now. It's getting dark and they…just shot at you and left?"

"Yes," Brody confirmed, his frown so deep it created creases around his mouth. "Just ran off. Like cowards."

"Maybe…" Kate swallowed. "Maybe they just wanted whatever it was they got and that's it. They clearly don't *really* want to hurt us."

Brody's hazel gaze focused in on her, intense and

not at all interested in her suggestion. "They drove us into a ditch, and while those bullets just now might not have hit me, they were plenty real. You're going to need a new refrigerator for your kitchenette."

Her stomach dropped out. Presumably the refrigerator was the only thing that kept those bullets from hitting him. "Brody..." She almost reached out. She couldn't have even said what she wanted to do. Hug him? Touch him? It was all so silly.

She just had to put it all to an end. That's what Dad had said. "This is...too much. If it's this much trouble, this much danger to look for my father, to look into Stanley Music, we should stop."

"Stop?" Brody echoed, like he didn't understand the word.

"If we let it go..." She didn't want to let it go. She wanted to know and understand what was happening. Why her father was here and had left her. Standing there. No real explanation. No teary greeting on his part. A terse warning with *guns* and then gone. "I don't want..." She stopped herself from saying *I don't want you to be caught in the crossfire*. It was true, and she knew, deep down, he would never accept that as a reason. He wouldn't consider himself in danger.

But she believed her father, that Brody would be, if he pushed this. It was her problem. Her mystery. Her father. Even her threat.

"I don't want to be in danger for these answers. That's not what I signed on for. I just wanted to know where he went, but if it's going to put me in danger, I don't want answers. It's been ten years without them. Better to just…let it go."

He stared at her for a very long time before he spoke. "Is that really what you want to do?"

She met his gaze. She had the horrible feeling she was disappointing him, which was absurd on a number of levels. Number one, she was saving him so it didn't matter what he thought. Number two, why should his opinion matter? She'd had to stop caring about what everyone thought a very long time ago.

He sighed before she could answer, put his hand on her shoulder. Oh so gently. "I know you're afraid, Kate. You have every right to be, and it's certainly nothing to be embarrassed about."

She wanted to laugh. She felt plenty of embarrassment over a lot of things, being afraid of this situation was hardly one of them. Car crashes and gunshots? Yeah, she wasn't embarrassed to be scared.

Still, better he read it that way than to understand what had really happened.

He squeezed her shoulder. "I promised I'd protect you, and I don't break my promises."

Now she really was going to cry. No. *No.* She'd already cried in front of him today. She was going to be strong and figure this out. She forced herself to smile. To put her hand over his and pat it in a friendly manner. "I'm sure you don't. You're a very good man." It physically hurt to say the next bit. "But I'm not your responsibility, Brody. I don't want this. It's more than I bargained for." She sucked in a breath, let it out. As she did, she took a step away from him, so his hand fell off her shoulder. She maintained eye contact no matter how much it hurt. "I'm done. I quit."

BRODY WAS SURE it took a full minute, maybe two, for the words to penetrate enough to make sense. *Quit?*

"Without answers? Without closure?" he said, because surely…surely that wasn't who she was. She was just scared. Shaken up. She'd find her backbone again and see this through.

Something flickered in her expression. "Yes." She said that so certainly, but her eyes told a different story. Conflict.

She wasn't sure at all. He wanted to press her, but he forced himself to keep his mouth shut. He'd just been shot at. He was used to that kind of thing, and honestly it wasn't so bad when it was just a coward trying to escape. Much worse when someone was determined to end your life.

But Kate wasn't used to gunfire. She was sheltered. He'd back off for tonight. Let her think they'd called it all off and that she was safe. If they could get home tomorrow, get her head checked out, they'd have a new discussion.

Or he'd tuck her away somewhere safe and handle it.

She couldn't possibly let it go. She just needed some time to accept or believe he'd keep her safe. That was all right. He had to remember he was dealing with a civilian, not a soldier.

"All right, Kate," he said at length, struggling to find a neutral tone. "If that's what you want."

She nodded firmly. "It is."

He tried to smile, but wasn't sure the movement of his face muscles made it even halfway there. He felt a bit frozen and awkward. Strange feelings for a man like him.

"Well, we're still stuck here tonight," he offered, searching for something to say. Some way to distract himself from the strange, crushing disappointment that had wound itself around his lungs. "New Year's Eve."

"I'll make some ashcake," she said, just a shade too desperately.

"No offense, but that doesn't sound very appealing."

She laughed, still that desperation in her tone, but he let her lecture him about ashcakes and she seemed to settle back into herself. He left the cabin as it was—table upended in front of the window with an assortment of heavier objects weighing it down. The front door was locked, not barricaded, but he'd keep an eye on it. He didn't plan on sleeping tonight.

Maybe the men today had run away. Their interest seemed to be information over hurting anyone, but that didn't mean things would stay that way. Still, he'd make sure it seemed like he'd put it away. Like it wasn't weighing on him.

He smiled as she handed him a plate with this...ashcake on it. "Well, it doesn't look like ash."

She rolled her eyes at him as she sat in a chair next to him, close to the fire, her own little cake on a plate in her lap. "I told you it's not *ash.* It's completely enclosed and *cooked* in the ash."

"Right, right."

Despite the rickety old construction—the snow and the fire worked to keep the cabin cozy. It didn't feel half as rustic as he'd anticipated. Much nicer than sleeping in a desert hunting a terrorist leader, that was for sure.

He studied her out of the corner of his eye. She was… fidgety. In a way, it was a positive. She wasn't acting like she was in a lot of pain or that she was dizzy or feeling any other adverse effects from the concussion. He needed to change her bandage, but he figured he'd let her eat her cake first.

Maybe he could find some way to put her more at ease. "I know that people shooting guns off isn't exactly a day at the park."

Her gaze went very…*imperious*, and she straightened in her chair. "A day at the park? No, we call gunshots and break-ins and all that…" She waved her hand in the general direction of the fort building. "We call *that* a day at the movies."

"It was just an attempt to get away. If they'd really wanted to hurt me, they would have—"

"Is this supposed to make me feel better?" she interrupted on a shocked demand.

She had a point, and since she did, he grinned and went for a joke. "Care about me, Kate?"

"I'm very grateful," she said solemnly, holding his gaze.

Not quite the answer he wanted, strangely enough. But probably best for both of them. "Probably be a good idea to switch out that bandage on your head."

"New bandage to ring in the New Year. *Woo.*" She wiggled her fingers unenthusiastically in the air, which made him grin.

He got up from the chair to retrieve the first-aid kit.

"I should look at your back, too. I should have looked before all this. Oh, Brody, you're probably in pain. I'm sorry, I—"

He put his hand on her shoulder so she didn't jump out of her chair to start fussing over him. "I'd let you know if it was a problem. No point in taking unnecessary risks out of pride. Now sit still."

She frowned, but did as she was told while he gently removed the adhesive holding her bandage in place.

She nibbled on her bottom lip and he had to work very hard to keep his mind focused on the task at hand. Her cut. Her bump. Her *concussion.* The cut had scabbed over, but the bump was still awfully big. "No headaches, dizziness, or anything else out of place?"

"Not really. My head hurts, but it's more a throbbing right there on the bump rather than something I'd call a headache."

"Good." He put on a new bandage, wondered if he should have had her ice that bump. Too late now. Get through tonight and ideally they'd get her to a doctor tomorrow. "All set."

She stood. "Your turn, then," she said, firmly, pointing at the seat.

"It's—"

"You can't ring in the New Year with a bloody old bandage. It's bad luck," she said, managing to keep a straight face despite the fact she was making stuff up. She looked at her watch. "You've only got ten minutes left."

He supposed there was no point in arguing. He'd make it fine another day or so with the same bandage, but if it made her feel better. He'd shrugged out of his coat earlier as the fire had warmed up the cabin, so he only needed to pull off the sweatshirt and thermal layers and sit so she could reach his back.

She made a distressed sound. “Brody.” Her fingertips gingerly touched his shoulder—much higher than that scrape. “I should have done this this morning. Hours ago. You’ve bled clean through—even your thermal.”

“But not my sweatshirt.”

She let out a frustrated breath. “Stay put.” She moved around the cabin—boiling snow again, coming up with some kind of rag. He couldn’t tell if she was more irritated at him for being this bad off, or more irritated at herself for not thinking to change the dressing on his wound.

He was betting on more irritated with herself, which made him feel…guilty, he supposed. “I’ll get checked out tomorrow.” If it really did need stitches, Dunne would no doubt stitch him up whether he wanted to be or not. “I promise you, it’s fine.”

“I promise you, I can see it better than you can and it isn’t *fine*. Maybe it’s not going to kill you, but it’s not *fine*. Now sit still. I’m going to wash it up and then rebandage it.”

“Yes, ma’am.”

She was quiet for a while, washing his back with her little rag, while one small hand rested on his back as if for balance. As if he was her anchor.

Clearly, he’d lost too much blood if he was thinking in such ridiculous metaphors.

“Did you get *all* these scars in the military?” she asked softly, with that same note of distress. Like she was worried for him, when those scars were so old he hardly remembered which ones came from where. At least the ones on his back.

He opened his mouth to make a joke about her undue interest in his scars, but in the end he found he really just wanted to tell her the truth. "Most. I was a boy left to my own devices, so I managed to scrape myself up some before I joined."

"How many years were you in the military?"

"Enlisted the minute I could. Deployed as often as I could."

"Didn't want to be home?"

"Not in the least, and it was a cost-free way—more or less—to get the hell out and do something worthwhile."

"So, why'd you stop if you were doing something worthwhile?"

The urge to tell her the truth was surprisingly strong. He couldn't, of course, but it was strange to come to the moment and *want* to. He'd always figured it'd be an easy enough secret to keep. After all, everyone important in his life knew, because everyone important in his life had been there.

Kate wasn't…important, exactly. *That* wasn't why he wanted to tell her. Not at all. It was because…. Well, if he told her, surely she'd trust him to handle this situation with her father. She'd understand he wasn't your average soldier. Or even above average. He'd been exceptional in every way. The only reason he was here instead of bringing down more terrorist groups was because he'd become too much of a target for doing just that. All because some idiot had pushed the wrong button.

Regardless of the whys, he was a target the military couldn't risk—not because of his life, but because of what he knew.

That was why he wanted to tell her. Because it would help. Not for any other reason.

But he couldn't, and now he'd waited a very long time to answer, which meant he needed something stronger than, *I guess I just felt like I was finished.* "Dunne was hurt." Which he supposed was the simplest, most truthful way he could explain it. "For the first time it made more sense to be stateside and civilian than enlisted and deployed."

"I don't understand how you can be so close to your brothers if you were alone as a kid."

He smiled a little. "That's because you don't have brothers."

She sighed, and it sounded sad, but she smoothed the bandage down on his back and then patted his shoulder. "All done."

He stood and turned to face her. She picked up his shirts. "You've ruined your shirt," she said, holding the gray thermal that now had a bloodstain on it—more blood than he would have anticipated—around the tear. No doubt Dunne would get some joy out of stitching him up, which Dunne could use.

"It'll do," he said, plucking the shirt out of her hands. He didn't wince as he pulled it on, only because she was studying him so intently.

With *interest*. If nothing else, she liked the look of his body and he found himself far too pleased that she did. But then she frowned. "You shouldn't be moving so much. You'll bleed through another bandage just overnight. Here." She took his sweatshirt and opened the neck hole and held it out to him—like he was a small child who needed to be dressed.

It was…sweet. A mothering kind of gesture he'd certainly never been offered in all his life. So, he bent forward and let her settle the sweatshirt over his head and then pull his arms through the sleeves.

"There," she said, giving a firm nod as if she was trying to convince herself all would be well. She gave his chest a pat, and then her hand just kind of *rested* there. And she stared at her hand on his chest like she wasn't quite sure what to do about it.

He covered it with his own. She inhaled sharply and then just sort of held her breath. He should let her hand go, certainly not turn it so he could read the time on her watch. Certainly not let the pad of his thumb stroke the inside of her wrist while he did so.

She let out that breath she held, a shuddery sort of sound. She didn't pull her hand away and it *was* New Year's Eve. Almost midnight.

He could kiss her. It was tradition. Good luck. Nothing more.

She looked up at him, the rise and fall of her chest a mesmerizing cadence to the moment. It was just New Year's Eve, that was all. And she didn't back away. If anything she leaned toward him.

So, he took the hand she was still holding and settled it on his waist, slid his own arm around her, pulling her closer. He took his sweet time—because it was enjoyable, because it gave her the chance to back away if she should want to.

But she didn't. So, he lowered his mouth to hers. He'd meant to make it simple. A brush of lips. Nothing more. Something that wouldn't reach inside him and rearrange everything, but that seemed to be all Kate was capable of when it came to him.

Because he lingered there at her mouth—soft and sweet, like spring in the middle of all this winter. And she held onto him, like she didn't want him to go anywhere. Which was fine with him. Right here was *more* than fine with him.

He slid his hand down her back, pulling her closer, so their bodies could touch, mold, melt. But she jolted there in his arms—in surprise more than alarm, because she didn't pull her mouth away from his. But it was enough of a lurch that Brody found about two brain cells to rub together and eased his mouth away from hers.

She was staring up at him with those big brown eyes like she didn't know *what* to do. *How* to react. Clearly, she felt very out of her depth, and Brody didn't really know how to make that right.

"Happy New Year," he managed, because he didn't have the slightest idea what to do about this except create some distance.

"Yeah, right. Happy..." she said, her voice just a faint echo.

He very carefully eased her back. "You should get some sleep, Kate. I'll watch the fire."

She nodded, blinked, then turned away and crawled into that sad little bed. He settled himself into his chair for a very long *uncomfortable* night.

Chapter Thirteen

Kate didn't sleep well. How was somebody supposed to sleep well after they'd been kissed like *that?* Surely not every kiss in the world would rock a person off their axis.

Not that she would know as that was the one and only time she'd been *really* kissed. Tim Fletch had put his overly moist mouth on her in the sixth grade, but Zara had pulled him off and punched him for her.

Always have someone else fight your battles, don't you, Kate? Not this time. Kisses or not. Confusion or not. She would not allow Brody to be caught in the crossfire of her own problems. If she had any New Year's resolutions, that was it.

Which meant she couldn't kiss Brody again. Not that he probably would. He'd just kissed her because it was New Year's. That was all. He wasn't really *interested.*

What if he is really interested?

Her stomach swooped because lonely girls who'd been isolated and shunned since the age of sixteen *had* to develop excellent imaginations, and Brody felt like some culmination of every fairy tale she'd ever dreamed up. Strong and handsome. Gentle and kind. Good all the way through. Protective and self-sufficient. She wasn't sure how he could be real, but she had to get it through her head that no matter how real he was, he wasn't for her.

Most especially *now*. She had to keep him far away from anything to do with her father.

When it was finally a decent hour to get up, she tried to creep out of bed, assuming he'd fallen asleep in his chair. But he was sitting there, eyes tracking her movements in the murky dark of morning in the cabin.

She blinked at him, her thoughts fracturing in a million different directions. Except the one she really couldn't entertain. *Couldn't we kiss some more?*

"You didn't sleep," she said, sounding strangled even to her own ears.

"Here and there." He smiled and held up his phone. "One of my brothers should be here any minute. They drove Zara's truck over, far as they could, then used a snowmobile to get the rest of the way. They'll take us back to the truck and then we'll head back to the ranch."

The ranch. Then home. This whole...thing was over. Which was good, what with his severe cut and her concussion. Doctors and home. Her mother. Life, back to normal.

And somehow finding a way to keep Brody out of her family drama. Because he wouldn't. He wouldn't just back off. She'd really have to convince him he needed to let it go.

She swallowed. It figured, didn't it, she finally had a man in her life—sort of—who she'd like to keep there, in a variety of different ways, but she had to push him out. For his own good.

"That's great. You really need to get your back checked out."

He stood, slowly. Somehow, even though he'd just sat in that uncomfortable chair all night, he looked perfectly rested. Even though he had that awful cut on his back, which she kept forgetting because he moved as if it didn't bother him at all.

And he'd kissed her. Really kissed her. Of his own free will. Not only to make her feel better. Even if he did it because of New Year's Eve, it was still at least kind of because he wanted to.

"We should pack up," he said gently.

Which was when she realized she was just standing there, staring at him. "Right. Yes." She jumped into action, moving probably more quickly than she needed to. But she could feel his eyes on her as she flitted about, packing up her stuff, putting the cabin back to rights.

Once she was satisfied, and had her bags over by the door, she slapped her hands together. "Well, I hope you enjoyed your trip back to 1872." She smiled up at him like she would to any fort visitor. Or tried. He was staring at her a little too intensely, standing a little closer than she'd thought.

"I did," he said, very seriously. So seriously her heart fluttered and she didn't look away from him like she should.

"Gunshots notwithstanding, I suppose."

"Seems in keeping with the frontier vibe," he said with a shrug. He stepped closer. So they were almost toe to toe. And she should step back. Look away. Because he was holding her gaze the same way he had last night and she knew what came next now.

But she *wanted* it.

No matter how her rational brain told her to stop, she didn't. When he lowered his mouth to hers, she kissed him back. Wound her arms around his neck. If last night had been an introduction, a test, this was something like a detonation.

He held her tight against his body. His mouth did things to hers she'd only ever *read* about. It was as amazing as all those romance novels said. So, she held on for dear life, and met all that fire with her own—as untested as it might be. Dimly, she realized the door behind her back was…vibrating. Someone was…knocking.

She pulled back a little, trying to blink herself back to reality. But Brody's mouth had moved down her neck and, *oh, wow*.

But someone was pounding on the door and yelling Brody's name.

Kate cleared her throat, gave him an ineffective push. "Brody."

"Hmm?"

"I think your brothers are here."

His head came up, his eyes cleared and he scowled at the door—someone was definitely on the other side, pounding on it and calling out his name.

"About the kind of timing they'd have," he muttered darkly, then gently moved her to the side so he could pull the door open.

Landon was on the other side. He took in Brody's

thunderous expression, then looked at her. Kate didn't know what he saw, but his mouth curved into a grin.

Kate didn't even have it in her to be embarrassed. Brody had kissed her. No countdowns to midnight in sight. Like he wanted to. Like he *liked* to.

It left her dazed at best.

"Well, let's get y'all loaded up," Landon said. He had the hint of a southern drawl, looked nothing like Brody. Or Cal, for that matter. Or Jake. Landon was fair—blond-haired and blue-eyed. He had a similar sturdy build, but his frame was lankier, less compact.

Even though Brody had said they weren't fully biologically related, Kate had to wonder if all this *brother* talk was something born of the military. At least for Brody. What he'd told her about her childhood sounded lonely and bleak.

Familiar.

People showing up to help this way was *not* familiar.

But that's what was happening. Brody and Landon carried everything and waited for her to lock up. There were two snowmobiles waiting—one empty, presumably Landon's. And one with a driver covered from head to toe in winter gear. If Kate had to guess, she'd say it wasn't Cal. And since it couldn't be Jake, it had to be Dunne or Henry. Based on Dunne's injury, which she knew nothing about except that he walked with a limp, she'd guess the driver was Henry.

Brody helped her onto the snowmobile behind Landon. "We'll talk at the house," he said in her ear.

Talk.

Talk about *what*? But he was climbing behind Henry

and then they were zooming off. The white was so blinding Kate had to close her eyes until they slowed to a stop. Waiting for them was a truck.

Kate blinked at the driver.

"I know it's a hardship, but you're going to have to let go, sweetheart," Landon said good-naturedly.

"Sorry," Kate muttered, her eyes still on Zara as she managed to climb off the snowmobile. The men were handling her bags and loading the snowmobiles up on the trailer the truck was pulling. Kate stood in the middle of it, not sure what to do or say.

Zara had been her best friend, but Zara had always had a very clear sense of wrong and right. What should be done and what shouldn't. Amberleigh and Dad's disappearance had meant Kate was *wrong*. For ten years, she had been *wrong* in Zara's eyes.

Kate was tempted to tell her to shove her help where the sun didn't shine. But Zara would probably laugh at that, not be offended.

"Come on," Brody said, taking her gently by the elbow. "You okay?"

Kate nodded and let him pull her to the truck. Zara climbed into the driver's seat without a word, and Kate and Brody climbed into the back. He was comically cramped in the narrow back seat, knees practically at his elbows once Landon got in. Henry climbed in the passenger and then they were off.

In silence, they drove to the Hart Ranch. Kate got the feeling Landon *wanted* to say something, but didn't have a clue where to start with all the different kinds of tensions layering the air.

The roads were clearly still bad. Zara drove slow and carefully, skidding a few times but holding the truck on the road with white knuckles and gritted teeth.

When she pulled up to the ranch, there was a sense of relief that they'd made it. Kate knew she should thank Zara as they got out of the truck, but honestly the only thing she could concentrate on was escape.

She stepped into the bitterly cold snow and gritted her teeth against it. She moved around the truck, finding Brody and Landon taking her bags out of the truck like they were going to take them inside. She couldn't let them do it.

"I really appreciate everything, Brody, but I should head home. I don't have a car, and I know the roads are bad, but the truck got through all right. Or I could maybe snowmobile over. I could ask Zara if you'd prefer, but—"

Brody was shaking his head. "You can't go home, Kate."

"But—"

He nodded at Landon and Landon headed inside after Zara and Henry, leaving her and Brody alone in the yard. Brody put his hand on her shoulder.

"I think you should stay with us for a day or two, just until we can be sure those guys aren't coming back. Zara spends the night a lot since Jake got shot, and Hazeleigh could spend the night, too, if it'd make you feel more comfortable. But… I can't let you go home just yet. Not until we know who was shooting at us."

"We don't *have* to know that," Kate said, and knew

she sounded overly desperate. "If they don't shoot anymore."

"But we don't know they won't," Brody said earnestly. Sweetly, almost. Protectively, definitely.

Of course she'd somehow find her way into kissing a guy who was earnest and protective, and her father's disappearance would get in the way. Or reappearance in this case. That *was* the story of every relationship in her life, wasn't it?

And she couldn't argue with Brody. Because in order to really prove that she was safe, she'd have to tell him the truth about talking to her father. Then he might believe she wasn't in direct danger anymore, but she didn't really think he'd back off. No matter what he did with that information, it would put him in a danger she couldn't stand the thought of him being in.

So, she had to go along with this. Force herself to lay low at the Hart Ranch for a bit, and when no one came after them, he'd let her go. He'd let *it* go. He had to.

BRODY CHALKED UP the wary way Kate looked at the house to all her history with Zara. He couldn't help but think maybe some close quarters had the potential to heal that rift or soothe it over. Zara had been the one to encourage him to help Kate, after all. There were clearly some unresolved feelings between the two women, and if Kate stayed put a few days, maybe these were ones she could resolve.

As a bonus she'd be safe, and maybe he could find the answers for her. She was scared to get them, that much was for sure. But that didn't mean she was safe if she *didn't*. He didn't want to scare her with that fact, so he'd handle it.

He led Kate inside, took her up to his room. "You can sleep in here tonight."

"Is this your room?"

"I'll take the couch." He put her bags down. "I'm going to go see about a doctor doing some kind of virtual appointment with you, and—"

"What about your back?"

"I'll have Dunne check it out. He has some medical experience."

Kate's frown deepened. "Some doesn't sound very reassuring."

"It is. I promise. Why don't you rest? It's been a long few days."

"You didn't sleep last night."

Last night. Which brought back thoughts of that kiss. Then the one this morning. Which wasn't why she was here, and it wasn't what he could allow himself to focus on right now.

No matter how much he wanted to.

The color rose on her cheeks and her eyes were on his mouth. She was thinking about it too.

He had to get out of here. Quick. "Just lie down for a bit," he said. Or instructed. He wasn't sure, because he got the hell out of there before he did something that would distract him from his mission.

Because figuring out who'd shot at him and what was going on with her father was definitely his mission.

He went to find Landon to discuss anything he might

have found on Stanley Music. He'd get around to Dunne and his back eventually.

Kate wanted to back off, and he understood. But she didn't understand Landon could find things without anyone knowing he'd found them. She didn't realize the lengths he and his brothers could go to keep her safe.

And he couldn't let her know, but he could help her. Even if she thought she didn't want his help.

He grimaced, because he felt a bit like Cal. High-handedly making decisions for her, without her knowledge. He wasn't going to keep her in the dark forever. Just…until she was ready to face this.

He didn't feel any *better* about it, but that didn't stop him. He found Landon in the kitchen, drinking coffee.

"Headed back out to help Cal with the cows," he said. "Zara's talking to some doctor in town to see if he can come out and take a look at Kate."

Brody nodded. "Anything on Stanley Music?"

"Haven't had much time, but I did some poking around. Whatever it is, it's got the kind of security walls that don't make sense for a *piano* company. I'll be able to dig further once I've got some more time."

Brody nodded. He wanted to push, but a blizzard meant other things came first. "What can I do?"

Landon's eyebrows raised. "Have yourself checked out."

Brody frowned. "What do you mean?"

"I've known you too long, seen you hurt too many times. I also saw that wreck of yours—I played down the damage to Cal. You're welcome. But I know something's wrong with you."

"Just a scrape on my back."

"So, you're basically bleeding to death?" Landon returned with a grin. He nodded to the door to Dunne's bedroom that also served as a mini medical center as needed. "He's waiting for you."

Brody hedged. "Got a few things yet to take care of."

"I'm sure you do. But you're going in there if I have to wrestle you in. And since I know you're injured, I know where to hit."

It *would* be a draw usually—a wrestling match. He and Landon were evenly matched, and rarely got the better of one another.

But Landon could be mean when he wanted to be, and he'd use Brody's injury against him to get what he wanted.

Brody sighed and went to Dunne's door. He knocked, then stepped inside.

The room was bright for a change, curtains drawn back. It was a sparse room, military clean as Dunne was a lifer—his father had been military too.

In the corner of the rather large room that Brody assumed had once been some kind of parlor, was a medical setup. Clean, efficient and prepped.

"Sit," Dunne said.

So Brady sat.

Out of all of them, Brody worried about Dunne the most. Or maybe it was a tie with Cal. They both held tight to the idea they could control *everything*. When everything about their lives these days made it very clear they could not.

When Dunne ordered him to take off his shirt, Brody did so.

The cursing he heard Dunne utter was the most he'd heard him say in almost six months. So maybe he'd bless the injury, even if he didn't bless the pain.

"Needs stitches," Dunne muttered.

"I figured," Brody said on a sigh.

Chapter Fourteen

Kate didn't do resting well. Especially here in Hart house, a place she'd spent many a childhood hour with her friends. All of whom were either dead or not so much friends anymore.

She didn't want to be here. She wanted to be home. Alone. Where she could deal with everything. On her *own*. Like she'd been doing for the past ten years.

But there was no way to get home.

Maybe if she asked Zara, Zara would drive her. Surely Zara would want her gone. Yes, that's just what she'd do. She plugged in her phone and changed her shirt since she had an extra sweatshirt in her bag.

Before she could do anything else, Zara barged in. No knock. Typical.

She had a phone to her ear. "Are you dizzy?"

"What? No."

"No dizziness. Swelling, but lucid. What day is it?"

"What?"

Zara rolled her eyes. "What day is it?"

"New Year's Day," Kate replied, crossing her arms

irritably. So like Zara to just barge in and make demands.

"Yup, she's good. Okay." Zara made a few more assenting noises, offered a thanks, then put the phone in her pocket. "Doctor says you're good. Rest. You can take acetaminophen if your head hurts. Any development of new symptoms, or if that swelling doesn't go down in a few days, you should either go in or call, depending on the road conditions."

"Fantastic," Kate muttered.

"Yeah, I saw that truck. You're pretty lucky."

"I feel like the end of a damn rainbow."

Zara *almost* cracked a smile. "I'm, uh, going to make dinner. You want to help?"

"*You're* making dinner?"

"I can cook."

"I know you *can.* You hate to, though."

Zara shrugged and waved Kate to follow. "The guys all take turns, but I've been picking up Jake's since I've been spending most nights here. Most of the time I have Hazeleigh come over and take my turn for me, but she's eye-deep in some project for Mr. Field she can do from the cabin."

"Right, well, how about you just drive me home instead? Then I won't be a burden."

Zara studied her at the top of the stairs. "You were shot at."

"No, *Brody* was shot at."

Zara rolled her eyes and headed down the stairs. "Brody can handle that."

"I know he was in the military, but—"

Zara stopped suddenly, sent her a quizzical look. "He told you that?"

Kate winced. He'd told her no one could know that, didn't he? She hadn't thought Zara would count, or maybe she *hadn't* thought.

"I mean, I *know* because Jake told me," Zara continued, leading Kate to the kitchen. "So, don't feel bad that you said it. I'm just surprised he told you as they don't really like telling anyone."

"He certainly didn't tell me much."

"No, he wouldn't." Zara moved to the fridge and began pulling out ingredients. "Sit down, concussion girl, you can chop."

Kate was by far a better cook, but she didn't see much point in arguing with Zara, who set a cutting board and some vegetables in front of her. "Chop away."

Kate just grunted and went to work. They worked mostly in silence, Zara standing at the counter, Kate sitting at the table. When someone broke the silence, Kate was just as surprised by Zara speaking as she was by what she said.

"I can't make up for ten years."

Ten years. Kate fought back the wave of sadness and focused on anger. "Probably couldn't hurt to *try*," Kate muttered.

Another silence followed, and Kate figured that would be that. But Zara sighed.

"I never hated you, Kate. I hated...everything that happened."

Kate looked up at Zara, who was frowning down

at the chicken she was cutting into pieces. "You had a funny way of showing it."

"Well, I've never been any good at grief, or sympathy, or… Well, you know me." She shrugged and dumped the chicken into a skillet.

Kate sighed and got to her feet. She went to where she knew they kept the spices, pulled out a few and began to season the chicken standing shoulder to shoulder with her ex-best friend. Who was putting out an olive branch for the first time in a decade.

Kate wanted to be harder. Angrier. But she knew Zara, and olive branches weren't frivolous. She wouldn't—couldn't—offer one unless she felt really miserable about what had happened.

"I didn't try either," Kate muttered.

"You shouldn't have had to."

"No, but… Look, we were sixteen. We sucked."

Zara laughed. "Yeah, we did. And so did it. But… I still should have been there. Your mom was difficult even before this, and I…left you to her. Same as leaving you to the wolves."

"Maybe," Kate agreed. "But you had your own wolves."

"Yeah, well…" Kate went and got the vegetables and brought them to the skillet. She handed the full cutting board to Zara and Zara slid them into the pan.

"Find me a lid."

Zara did as told.

Then they stood there and watched the meal cook. Kate couldn't say they'd just absolved ten years of hurts, but it was a step, she supposed.

"Look, do you think you could drive me home? I know Brody thinks I'm in danger, but I swear I'm not."

"Car accidents and shootings aside?"

Kate blew out a frustrated breath. "I don't want to be his responsibility. I don't want him… Even if he could handle whatever, I don't *want* him to."

Zara frowned at her. "Brody's a good guy."

"I know he is." Way too good, in fact.

"If anyone can help you, Kate, it's him. It's the whole lot of them."

"Maybe I don't want any help."

"I guess that's fair." Zara studied her, and she shouldn't be able to have any insight after ten years of distance, but Kate had a bad feeling she understood all too well. "But do you not want it because you don't, or because after ten years of getting the shaft, you don't trust help when it's offered?"

Kate stared at Zara, because that statement caused an awful pain in her chest. She wanted to protect Brody, she *did*, but maybe…maybe in part because she just wasn't sure his help would go right. Maybe she was a little sure it would end in disaster because, yes, for ten years no one had tried to help.

"Been there. Done that. So I recognize the signs," Zara said quietly. "But Jake just kept being there, helping me out. Because… I don't know, they just have to. It's who they are. They *have* to do the right thing, even when it's not *their* right thing. I don't know how else to explain it."

Kate knew Zara didn't have any clue how much that twisted the knife of guilt she was already impaled by.

"I can't take you home. I trust Brody's judgment on this. You aren't safe."

"Maybe *he* isn't safe."

Zara blinked, studied Kate with a scrutiny Kate did *not* appreciate, but couldn't avoid. Because she wasn't that mysterious. She hadn't changed *that* much.

"First, I think you underestimate what Brody is capable of. I've seen it firsthand, and you know not much impresses me. Second, he wouldn't want you protecting him, for a wide variety of reasons." Zara reached out and touched Kate's shoulder—not something Zara was much on doing even when they had been friends. "If you have any feelings for Brody, any at all, you need to tell him the truth. Whatever the truth is. He deserves the truth, and he can handle it. The truth *and* whatever this is."

Kate pulled back from Zara's hand. "The truth is we'd all be a lot better off if I stopped looking into my father's disappearance."

Zara nodded. "Then you need to tell him that, and tell him why. Because trust me, no matter what Brody says out loud, he's going to get to the bottom of this for you. The only way to stop him is the truth."

Kate blinked, her entire body going cold. She wanted to deny what Zara was saying, but Brody had given in so easily. He was also making her stay here. Zara was right.

He'd say he'd given it up. And keep going. Not in a duplicitous kind of way, exactly. But because of whatever it was inside of him that made him need to protect. Help.

She should be irritated by that, instead of feeling even more tangled up about how much she liked him. "I need to talk to him."

Zara nodded behind Kate and Kate turned to see Brody and Dunne standing in a doorway that Kate knew went to the main floor bedroom.

Kate sucked in a breath, then marched over to him and grabbed him by the arm. "Come on." She pulled him out of the kitchen, ignoring the fact Dunne and Zara were likely watching them go with avid interest.

It didn't matter. The only thing that mattered was getting him to stop. She dragged him all the way back to his room. She closed the door behind her.

"You're still looking into it, aren't you?"

Brody's eyes widened, but he stuck his hands into his pockets and rocked back on his heels. "Well…"

"I told you to stop!"

"I know, Kate. But you have to understand, until we get to the bottom of this mystery, we don't know what that car accident or shooting was about. We don't know you're safe—no matter how much you want to be or insist you are."

She wrung her hands together. Maybe she could find a way to tell him the truth that would get him to back off. Get him to understand. She believed Zara. A lie wouldn't work. He'd get to the bottom of it.

So she had to go with a deeper truth. "You've made me an awful lot of promises, Brody. You shouldn't. I'm nothing to you."

"That isn't true. At all." He crossed to her, took her

wringing hands in his and held her gaze. "I told you, I like you, Kate." So serious. So honest.

"I know." Her hands stilled under his and she wanted to lean into him. She wanted to kiss him like they had this morning. See where it went—where it could go. She wanted to, far more than she should.

But she had to ignore the flutter in her heart. It would change her mind, and she couldn't. If he kept pushing, he would get *hurt*. No matter how strong or smart he was.

I think you underestimate what Brody is capable of, Zara had said. Zara, who never thought anyone was as strong or stubborn or determined as her. Maybe she could tell him and get him to back off and maybe… Maybe Brody knew what he was doing.

She blew out a shaky breath. She didn't want to take that chance—she didn't want *him* taking that chance.

He liked her…? He kept *saying* he liked her, and there was no reason to lie. No reason to kiss her the way he had. She couldn't manage a reason to make his kisses false, which only tangled everything more. "I almost wish you didn't like me," she managed.

He grinned, pulled her to him. "Almost."

She wanted to sink into that acknowledgment, but she couldn't allow herself. It wasn't right to let him kiss her and like her when she'd lied to him. She pushed at his chest. "Brody, there's something I have to tell you." She didn't know how else to do this. She knew he wouldn't want to kiss her anymore. And he also wouldn't let the thing with her father go. She got nothing she wanted if she told him the truth.

But she just *had* to. Because, like Zara had said, he wouldn't let up. Moreover, like Brody himself had said back at the cabin, it was the right thing to do.

KATE LOOKED SO DISTRESSED, it ate at him. Brody let her go, let her start to pace. She muttered a few things to herself, but Brody waited. She had something to say, so he waited.

No matter how he itched to touch.

"You can't go after my father. You can't look into Stanley Music. I know you want to. I know you think it's the right thing to do." She turned to face him, so heartbreakingly desperate. "Can't you trust me that it isn't?"

He didn't understand her fear. He tried, really. Tried to put himself in a civilian's place, where random gunfire might in fact scare them enough to back off. But she'd been so tenacious for ten years. He couldn't reconcile that with this.

Or the expression on her face. Scared and desperate. She had a right to be scared. More than a right. But he didn't understand the desperation. Like there was a very specific threat lodged at them when Brody wasn't even sure anyone *really* wanted them dead. Scared, yes. Hurt—maybe, and certainly if they wanted them hurt, that could lead to inadvertent death. But her behavior still didn't fully make sense to him.

The answers weren't written on her face, so he placed his hands on her shoulders. "It's not that I don't trust you, Kate. It's that I don't understand what's going on. What is this about? Really?"

Her face crumpled. Not into tears. More like she

couldn't hold the weight of something. She pulled away from his hands. She didn't start pacing again, but she backed away from him slowly, once again wringing her hands.

"Kate—"

"I saw my father," she blurted out, squeezing her eyes shut like she was afraid of a blow that would come after that confession.

But her words didn't make sense. "What do you mean?"

She sighed, opened her eyes, which were shiny with unshed tears he also didn't understand. "When you told me to lock myself in the cabin, he was there."

Brody thought there must be some kind of earthquake under his feet—it was the only explanation for feeling so suddenly off-kilter. "There. In the cabin. *With* you?"

She nodded.

"Why… Why wouldn't you have told me that? Where did he go?" He stepped toward her. He didn't know what emotions were swirling through him. Anger, and frustration, and a hurt that was out of place, for sure. "I could have followed. You should have yelled. You were *alone* with him?" he demanded.

"He just… He was there and he told me to stop looking into things. To let it all go."

"Oh, well, then let's give *up. Naturally,*" Brody said sarcastically. He felt guilty for being so scathing, but that only made him angrier. Why should he feel guilty? He'd been trying to help her and she'd… She'd just give up because her father showed up after a decade and out of nowhere and told her to?

"He said..." Kate cleared her throat. "Brody, he said he'd been protecting me, but he couldn't if I kept pushing. He said if you kept going after them, you'd *beg* for death." Some of that indecision, and sadness, and uncertainty hardened into sparks of anger. "How could I have told you knowing that you would have absolutely still gone after them even with a *death* threat leveled against you?"

Those words, unexpected and unique, stopped him in his tracks. Leaked all the anger, and frustration, and confusion out of him. "You're... You're trying to protect me." It was a very strange feeling, and it took him a moment—or maybe a few—to wrap his head around how out of sorts that made him feel.

He'd been fighting side by side with his brothers for years. They had each other's backs, and they'd certainly jump in front of a bullet for each other. In fact, had done so. But that wasn't...protection. That wasn't this.

She'd wanted to give up on ten years of looking for her father, not just because her father had said he wouldn't be able to protect her anymore if she kept pushing. No, the way Kate had said that made it seem secondary. Made it seem like the most important thing, the thing that would make her give it all up, was the death threat leveled at *him*.

"I'm sorry," she said, though it was a little stiff. "I just thought... He was very specific, Brody. Not just that you'd be killed, but that it would be...messy. He had two guns, and all this gear, and... I know you probably think you could handle it. Zara thinks you could handle it. Everyone thinks you could handle it and maybe you could. What do I know? Not a darn thing, except I couldn't live with it. You shouldn't be risking any of it for *me*."

He crossed the room. Maybe he should have kept the distance. He was off balance enough to make a mistake, but she looked so miserable and worried and he… He had to touch her. Assure himself this bizarre change of events was *real*.

"Why not?" he asked, taking her hands in his.

"What?" she asked, looking at their hands as if she didn't understand why he was touching her.

"Why shouldn't I risk it for you, Kate?"

She looked up at him, and he knew no one had really backed her up before. Her mother sounded terrible. Her friends had backed off. She'd been alone and surviving in her own way for a decade.

He knew what that was like, and how hard it could be to believe someone might want to stand by your side. To fight with you. He hadn't become *brothers* with his friends overnight. They'd all slowly had to learn to trust and believe in each other.

Because he knew, and understood, he wanted to give her…everything. Maybe if he stepped back and analyzed it, it didn't make any sense. But he didn't want to do that. He touched his mouth to hers, thinking it could be something light and sweet. Reassuring.

But he couldn't pull himself back. He wanted to hold onto her. To drown himself, and her, in this and in them. She melted into him, pliant, and he couldn't imagine anyone else ever belonging here in his arms the way she did.

He tangled his hands in her hair, and her hands wrapped around his biceps, clutching him closer to her. The kiss was a perfect, sweet world distinct from everything else going on around them, and he'd have been happy to stay here. Right here. Rather than deal with everything else.

But everything else always came calling, whether a person wanted it to or not. He sighed against her mouth, pulling himself slightly back. They needed space. They needed to focus on the task at hand.

But when he looked at her, all he could think about was how much he wanted her in his bed.

"I thought you'd be mad at me," she said, looking up at him, eyes clouded with desire even amidst all that confusion. "For lying."

"We all lie, Kate." He ran his hands down her arms. Wasn't he lying to her now, more or less? If he told her everything he'd done in his military career, wouldn't she believe that he could handle whatever her father leveled at him? But some lies were…necessary. Maybe. "I've just never had anyone lie *for* my safety before."

She still clutched his arms, looking up at him. But her expression went imploring. "If we stop, he'll just leave us alone. He's alive, that's enough for me to know. We don't need to know what bad thing he got himself caught in. I'm safe. You're safe. That's all that matters."

He wished that were true. Wished he could let her believe it were true. Agree and take her to bed.

But she was dead wrong, and if he didn't do something about it, they could both wind up dead.

"Kate, they keep taking information *you* have." He ran his hand over her hair. "At some point, they're going to wonder what you can prove even *without* the evidence they've stolen."

Chapter Fifteen

Kate wanted to drown in the warmth Brody's body provided, but his words were a cold reminder that her real life was something…twisted and ugly and confusing.

The only way she'd been able to survive it had been to withdraw into herself. Now she had Brody kissing her, and Zara apologizing. People rallying around her to help.

Brody kissed her temple. "Come on, let's go eat dinner."

She tried to smile as she nodded agreement, and she let him hold her hand on the way down to the kitchen. It was a reassurance she supposed. He hadn't taken any relish in telling her they'd come after her eventually, and he hadn't dropped the bomb and left.

He was here. He wasn't mad she'd lied. He'd been bowled over that she cared enough to protect him.

Maybe they were more alike than she'd thought, and maybe…that should give her some hope. Brody had grown up feeling alone, solitary. He'd made that clear. But he'd made a life with his brothers as an adult. Clearly excelled in the military. And when Dunne had been hurt, rallied together with his brothers to move here.

They took turns cooking, and apparently they all

ate together. When Brody pulled her into the kitchen, all five other brothers were in the room. Zara was still back by the stove, hopefully not ruining the dinner Kate had helped her start, while Henry stood next to her, filling cups with milk. Dunne and Jake were both sitting. Landon was sitting as well, but he had a computer in front of him he was tapping away on. Cal stood by the back door, looking grumpy—which Kate wasn't sure she'd ever seen him look anything but.

"How's the head, Kate?" Jake asked.

She managed to smile. "Good enough."

Brody ushered her into a seat, and he took the one next to her. Zara put the skillet on a trivet and a bowl of fruit next to it. Henry doled out glasses of milk, and Cal eventually sat next to Landon.

"You're in my seat," he muttered.

Landon grinned at him. "First come, first serve, buddy."

Zara handed out plates and silverware, then moved to sit next to Jake. Her hand trailed across his shoulder, and he scooted the chair next to him out for her. She handed him a napkin, he handed her the serving spoon from the fruit. It was an oddly mesmerizing dance. Zara had always been so fiercely independent. So resistant to any help. She'd done everything for everyone.

Now she was holding a man's hand under the dinner table.

Kate snuck a glance at Brody. He was looking at Landon's computer screen with a frown, but there was an ease to him here. Surrounded by his brothers, cramped together around a kitchen table Kate had eaten at as a child before the triplets' mother had died.

There'd been a similar vibe then. Family. Warmth. Chatter. Much different than Kate's own house, even before Dad's disappearance.

It was kind of amazing Zara had found a way to bring that back.

They ate, and Landon didn't put the computer away. Instead he pointed out things he'd found about Stanley Music, making Kate's stomach twist with anxiety.

Was she putting them all in danger?

"The security set up around any mention of this place is high tech. It's definitely not a music company. The piano thing is a front, but it'll take me some time to dig under the front without anyone figuring it out." Landon frowned at the computer screen while he took a bite of dinner.

Kate opened her mouth to tell him he didn't have to stick his neck out for her, but Brody silenced her with one clear disapproving look.

"I'll handle your chores tomorrow, give you more time."

Landon nodded, but Dunne shook his head. "You've got to give those stitches a few days to heal, cowboy."

Brody scowled.

"Welcome to the wounded crew," Jake offered, holding his glass up in mock salute.

"At the very least, Kate should stay here until we can be sure she's not in danger," Brody said firmly.

All eyes except Brody's turned to Cal. He was scowling, but based on what little Kate had seen of Cal Thompson, he was *always* scowling.

But there was something like an…ingrained chain of command, she supposed. They weren't waiting for permission, she didn't think. She couldn't imagine Cal refusing and Brody just shrugging and saying *okay, go home, Kate.* But they were waiting for…well, a fight.

As if sensing that, Cal changed his scowl. She thought maybe he was trying to smile, though it wasn't a very believable one.

"Of *course* she should stay. At your service, Kate."

Dunne snorted, Landon grinned and Brody looked torn between irritation and amusement.

This was the kind of family she'd always imagined during uncomfortably silent dinners with her parents. Not all happiness and light, but…real interaction. Connection. It was what she'd had with the Hart triplets. Before.

They ate the remainder of dinner, much of the conversation revolving around ranch chores—which had always been a Hart dinner-topic staple. Though Kate supposed this wasn't the Hart house or Hart Ranch anymore. It surprised her how well Zara had eased into that transition.

But she supposed it had something to do with the man who's hand she was holding under the table.

"Well, I've got a few things to go over. Thanks for dinner, Zar—"

Cal was already on his feet, but Zara was shaking her head. "You can't go yet," Zara said, standing. "Dessert." She turned her gaze to Kate. "Kate knows what she has to do to earn us dessert."

Kate's jaw dropped. "You can't be serious."

"Mom's rules. I *always* abide by Mom's rules."

It was strange how easy it was to fall into who they'd been before with each other—even though neither of them were who they'd been before. "Your mom would not be cool with you living with a guy before marriage."

Zara's grin widened as she lifted a shoulder. "I never minded a little of my mother's disapproval. *You* on the other hand…"

"Just what exactly are we witnessing here?" Landon stage-whispered.

"Kate has to play for us," Zara said. "Her choice of instruments, since she can play them all."

"Do we…*have* instruments?" Jake asked, genuinely perplexed.

Zara rolled her eyes. "You should really pay more attention to your own house, Jake." She pushed back from the table and Kate kept shaking her head.

"We are not little kids anymore."

"Fine. Enrage my mother's ghost. See how well you sleep tonight." Zara grinned, and Kate felt a matching one tug at her mouth.

Bittersweet, yes, but the sweet was starting to drown out some of that bitterness. Which was how about fifteen minutes later she was situated in the living room, Zara's late grandpa's fiddle in her hands. All the men gathered around for an impromptu concert.

Kate hadn't played in front of anyone in years, but music had always been her solace. She expected to be nervous, but once she started the song, it was like she was the only person in the room. Until she finished, and everyone applauded.

She gave a silly little bow, accepted the many compliments, flushing with the simple pleasure of sharing something she loved. Much like her job at the fort when she got to lecture people about her interests, but this was…different. More intimate.

As she walked upstairs, tired and ready to just *sleep*, she realized that thanks mostly to Zara, but also the Thompson brothers, for hours there, she'd forgotten about her father. About concussions and stitches and gunshots. She'd enjoyed her life, enjoyed other people.

She stepped into Brody's room—what had once been Amberleigh's when they'd been ten or eleven, before she'd made Hazeleigh switch with her so she had the room that could be easier to sneak out of.

But Kate didn't think of Amberleigh or Hazeleigh. She thought of herself. Kate Phillips. Who she'd always been, but had lost parts of. She liked this Kate, and the…future she seemed to have now.

She turned to face Brody who stood hesitantly in the doorway, and for some reason his uncertainty in this moment gave her courage. And a sense of…purpose.

"We really don't have to push this—the whole thing with my dad. Not just to protect anyone, Brody." She looked at him as he studied her. "I… Tonight was nice. It could just be…like this."

He nodded, and some of the tension in her shoulders unwound as he crossed the room to stand in front of her. "We can do that," he agreed, putting his hands over hers. "But how long does that last, Kate?"

She closed her eyes. "I don't care," she said, even though it was a lie.

He squeezed her hands like he knew her words were a lie. "You deserve answers, and I think you have the right to be sure none of this comes back to bite you later. If we see it through to the end, we get all that—and at the end of it all, I promise you, it can still be just like this."

She opened her eyes and looked up at his hazel ones. He really was *so* good, but she didn't think he understood how much she didn't want to ruin what she'd had tonight. "Do you know what it's like to feel like yourself for the first time in ten years?"

His expression took on an arrested look that softened into an understanding. "Yes. I do."

He understood, and that was just another thing she'd had too little of. And he was something she'd never had. Why shouldn't she take, while she could?

"You should get some sleep," he said, sounding raspy. Backing away, though he didn't turn for the door. Just took a step away from her.

She didn't want that. She took the step he'd retreated, reached out and touched his chest and held his gaze, filled up with all this old and new confidence. "Stay."

He froze, and she almost smiled at how carefully he held himself. "I can take the floor or..."

"Brody," she said, shaking her head. "Don't be thick-headed."

"I'm not. I'm trying to be…noble."

She grinned, because for a little bit of time today she'd felt like who she used to be. Before she closed up, closed in. She felt like… Kate Phillips. Not a pariah, or a loner. Just herself.

"Don't."

BRODY WOKE UP in the familiar bed of the Hart Ranch. He hadn't gotten used to calling it *his* bed, but if he woke up with Kate every morning, maybe he'd get there.

She was still fast asleep. Hair in disarray on his shoulder. He thought maybe there should be some guilt here, but he couldn't find it. Probably because he cared. Deeply. And he knew, no matter what, he'd do everything it took to give her answers, to keep her safe. To give her that same glow she'd had last night playing the fiddle.

Then again in his bed.

He slid out of bed, hoping not to wake her. She muttered something, rolled over and then was back to being fast asleep.

In his bed, in this new life he'd been building for himself. Outside the military.

Did he know what it was like to feel like himself for the first time in a decade—over a decade for him? More than he'd ever be able to put into words. And while some of that was the ranch, and the lack of structure the military had provided to constantly measure himself against as proof he was better than all he'd come from, the final piece, the *key* had been Kate.

Dressed, he crept out of the bedroom. He needed some coffee and a chat with Landon about Stanley Music, and Kate needed her sleep. He'd fill her in on whatever he found when she woke up.

Besides, he didn't have the first clue what to say to her if she woke up. It all felt a little…overwhelming. Too big for only the short time they had been together. He needed to be careful. They both needed to be careful. If they were, maybe something with some longevity would work out. But too hot, too fast was bound to scorch them both.

Coward.

Probably so.

He entered the kitchen, irritated with himself. Landon was at the kitchen table, his computer in front of him, a mug of coffee at his side. He smoothed out his expression and greeted Brody with a, "Good morning."

Brody poured himself some coffee, then took the seat next to Landon. "Anything new?"

"Bits and pieces, but nothing concrete. Stanley Music is definitely a front. For what and who? Still digging."

"You're sure no one knows you're digging?" Landon glared, clearly affronted. Brody held up his hands. "Kate's the one in danger of getting caught in the middle. We can't be too careful."

Landon's expression went surprisingly shrewd. "What's going on there?"

Brody shrugged, looking at his coffee rather than the odd air of disapproval on Landon's face.

Landon grunted. "You and Jake are as subtle as sledgehammers falling for—"

Brody whipped his gaze up, all warning.

Landon rolled his eyes and sighed. "Lovely young women."

"I live for the day you do anything with subtlety, Landon."

There was a moment—so quick, Brody wondered if he'd imagined it—where Landon's expression went grave. Then he grinned. "What's the point in being subtle?" He tapped his laptop. "Unless it's hacking related, of course. Look, I'll focus on this today. Zara said they're pretty well dug out of the blizzard. Looks like the roads are better today. Cal can't get too mad at me missing a day of chores."

"Except it's you, me *and* Jake missing chores."

"You know he's only grumpy because you both got hurt on his watch."

"His watch," Brody grumbled. "At some point he's going to have to learn we aren't his to watch anymore."

"Aren't you the one always telling me to give him time?"

"Yeah, yeah, yeah."

"There is one thing you could do, as long as the roads really are up for it and Dunne clears you to drive. I called the county office yesterday to check in on a business license, but they said I'd have to come down in person. If you can get a look at that license, there should be a name or maybe a shell company we can follow up on. You do that, I'll put in some chores so Cal can unclench."

"Yeah. Absolutely." Brody was already on his feet, ready to move.

"Make sure Dunne says driving's okay."

Brody nodded. He didn't *want* to, but he supposed it wouldn't hurt to ask. And if Dunne said no? Well, at least Brody would know he needed to sneak around.

But first, he needed to tell Kate… Well, maybe not everything. Enough. Something. She was enjoying feeling normal again, and if he could figure out her whole Dad thing himself, without her having to worry over it, well… Wouldn't that be good?

He found a clean mug, filled it and then retraced his steps back upstairs. When he slid into his room, Kate was sitting up in bed, running her hands through her tangled hair. She looked over at him sleepily.

"Morning. Brought you some coffee. Didn't put any cream or sugar in it, but I figured a pioneer woman knew how to take it black."

She smiled. "You'd be wrong, but I'm desperate enough not to care this morning."

He moved over and carefully handed it to her, then because he couldn't help himself, dropped a quick kiss to her mouth. He would rather sink into kissing her, coffee be damned, but he wanted…to fix everything for her too. The sooner he got to work, the sooner he could.

"I'm going to do some chores this morning. Ranch is kind of slammed from the blizzard."

Her eyebrows drew together. "I thought Dunne told you not to do any chores."

"Cal found me some lighter assignments that won't mess with my stitches."

"How can I help?"

"Sit tight."

She frowned. "I didn't grow up on a ranch, but I know a thing or two and…"

"Best if you sit tight," Brody reiterated. "You've still got to be careful of that concussion," he said, drifting his fingers over her bandage. "And Cal can be a grumpy SOB. Just rest. Maybe tomorrow you'll be up to some light chores. In fact, I'll work on him today. He'll have stuff for you to do tomorrow and he'll even think it's his idea. Nothing puts Cal in a better mood than something that's his idea."

"What am I supposed to do then?"

"Whatever you want. Rest. Relax."

Kate grimaced.

He took a seat next to her on the bed. "I wish I could take you to the fort so you could work, but it isn't safe. Not yet."

"No, I know." She shook her head and gave him a smile. "I'll figure something out. Maybe make a big lunch for you guys."

He took her hand and pressed his mouth to the top of it. "You'd be considered a god among us lowly mortals."

She snorted a laugh. "All right, then. Goddess it is."

Brody got up, wanting to get on the road. He had a good hour's drive to the county clerk's office.

"Brody, about last night…"

He froze, a strange dread creeping through him. Did she have regrets? Was this where she let him down easy?

"That was good, right?"

He turned, cupped her face with his hands, careful

not to jostle her into spilling her coffee. "Last night was great."

She grinned. "You'll spend the night with me again tonight?"

"Any night you want."

Chapter Sixteen

Kate was so bored she could scream. She'd managed to keep herself occupied daydreaming about Brody for a good hour. Then she'd gotten restless, and cleaned the kitchen, and made soup, which now simmered on the stove. She'd preprepared sandwiches to go with the soup. She'd even peeked in on Jake, who she *barely* knew, to see if he needed anything while Zara was out working.

But nothing really needed to be done, and she was in not-her-house with not-her-things. She messed around with the old fiddle, but even that couldn't hold her interest.

She needed a trip home. A few changes of clothes. Different shoes. Her laptop. She had most of the things to get her through a few days away from home, but a few days was up and she needed a refresher.

Besides, she never let herself go too many days without asking her mother if she needed anything. Maybe Mom wouldn't notice her absence, but Kate…felt guilty anyway.

She looked around the kitchen, then decided now

was as good a time as any. She pulled her phone out of her pocket and called someone she hadn't called in ten years. Zara.

"Hey, Kate. What's up?" Zara greeted.

Kate could hear the wind whipping in the receiver. Zara was out working, and Kate was *jealous*. It made this choice even more necessary. "Can I borrow your truck? Just going to run home and get a change of clothes and stuff. Maybe run into town for some dinner supplies. I made sandwiches for lunch because there wasn't anything really defrosted, but I'd like to make a hot dinner."

"It's Cal's turn to cook," Zara replied. "So if you're willing to take over so I don't have to have half-baked frozen pizza, I'm in. Brody okay with you taking off?"

Kate knew she shouldn't lie, but the fib came out of her mouth before she could stop herself. "Of course."

"Extra set of keys hanging up in the mudroom."

"Thanks."

"No prob."

Kate hung up, grabbed the keys, and then her purse, and was headed out for Zara's truck in no time. The crew would come back in for lunch in about two hours or so, so she had plenty of time. She'd be back to check on her simmering soup and set out the sandwiches before everyone was back.

She hummed to herself as she got in Zara's truck. This could be normal. This could be real life, and no matter what Brody had said about answers, Kate finally realized she didn't *need* them. Maybe it was seeing Dad that had done it. He was alive. He'd made a choice to leave.

Now she knew, and no matter what he was mixed up in, he'd made his own choice.

It was closure. Sort of.

Kate turned the key in the ignition, then sighed, a little kernel of guilt eating at her. What if Brody came in early and she was gone? Zara would know where she was, but he would worry first. Worry too much.

Which was nice, actually, someone to worry over her. But it meant she owed him…an explanation.

A text. A quick to-the-point text. Picking up some stuff at my house, and some groceries at the Mart. Be back before lunch.

She read it back to herself. Considered. Maybe she should just stay put. Wait for Brody and…

Oh, for heaven's sake, no one had tried to hurt *her*. They'd tried to hurt him. He was the one who should be worried. Maybe it would be like high school when she felt like she was being followed, but no one was going to shoot her for driving home.

She hit Send and began to head off the Hart Ranch. Her phone rang not two seconds later. She sighed and answered.

"Hello," she offered brightly.

"Damn it, Kate," Brody's voice growled. It echoed through the speaker. She even liked his voice. So low and commanding, regardless of the situation.

She kept her tone light and breezy. "Brody, it's just home. A trip to the Mart. I'll be back in no time."

"No trip to the Mart. Absolutely not. Go home."

She didn't know why it warmed her that he was treating the Hart place like *her* home. "Just a change of clothes. Pop in and say hello to my mother, and make sure she doesn't need anything. Brody, you can't keep me prisoner. I have to be able to do *something*."

There was a long fraught silence. Kate drove, and she paid attention. Waited for someone to jump out. A car to appear and follow her. Shots. But nothing.

"You can't treat me like I'm a frail doll," she said seriously. "Or in mortal danger *all* the time. That's overkill, and I think you know that. They've stolen from me, yes, but they haven't done more than that and follow me around a bit here and there."

"Here and there," he muttered disgustedly. "They ran us off the road."

"Us. Not me."

"Kate..."

She knew he wanted to argue more. She also knew he couldn't stop her, but she wanted him to understand. She needed him to. So, even though it was embarrassing to admit, she had to tell him.

"I spent an entire year of my life anxious and paranoid. In and out of the counselor's office. I wanted to see a therapist, Brody, because I couldn't control my thoughts. Mom wouldn't let me, so it was a hard-won fight to find some peace. I can't go back to that place. I can't do it again. I have to be able to live the way I've been living."

His silence took on a life of its own and Kate held her breath. This would be a sticking point. She couldn't constantly be babysat. She wouldn't constantly be fearful. Her father was out there, doing something shady, maybe, okay probably, but he'd been protecting her. Brody was protecting her by being careful looking into Stanley Music.

She just couldn't be sixteen again. She couldn't *feel* like that again. She wasn't sure she'd be able to crawl out, even as an adult with help available to her now. People who cared. Whatever therapist she wanted. She didn't know how to survive it twice.

"If you feel anything is wrong, you're being followed at all, *anything*. You call me," Brody said, sounding pained but he was giving her the space she asked for. "You call the police. I don't care, you do whatever you have to do to stay safe," Brody ordered.

Which was fine enough. She didn't want to die or be attacked. She just wanted a change of clothes. Some time alone to think. In her own space. "All right."

"Promise me."

"I promise. I don't have a death wish, Brody. I have plans tonight."

Het let out a low chuckle. "They better be with me."

"Of course."

Then he sighed. "I should probably confess something."

Kate parked Zara's truck on the road. Her mother would pitch a fit if a rusty old truck was parked in the drive, and it hadn't been shoveled anyway. She should do that. "What should you confess?" she asked, climbing out of the truck.

"I'm running an errand for Landon, trying to look at a business license for Stanley Music."

Kate stopped in her tracks. "Brody!"

"It's nothing."

"It's poking into things. They threatened you as much if not more than me. Turn around and go home now."

"How about this? We both do the thing we've set out to do that we lied to each other about, and then tonight we show each other just how sorry we are."

It was absurd. She should absolutely be furious with him, not walking toward her house, *smiling*. He'd lied.

Then told her the truth when she fessed up too. He hadn't had to. She would have never known the difference. Maybe that was a low bar, but it was her bar. She'd done the same more or less, hadn't she? "I hope you're very sorry."

"The sorriest. I might be sorry two or three times."

Which had her smiling all over again. She was probably pathetic, but she didn't *feel* pathetic. She felt as happy as she'd been in *years*. "All right, but you have to promise me the same thing—if anything feels wrong, you call for help."

"Yes, ma'am."

She sighed and tested out the words he'd said himself. "I'll see you at home."

"Soon enough."

She ended the call and slid the phone back into her pocket. She looked up at the house on the hill. It looked as dark and abandoned as it ever did. She'd learned to accept that she existed in a weird kind of living mausoleum to her father's memory—or disappearance or *whatever* went on in her mother's head.

But cohabitating with Brody in the historical cabin, and then the Hart house packed to the brim with people, she realized how *sad* it all was. Zara had said she'd left her to the wolves, because Kate's mother had always been cold and distant.

But the truth was, her mother had felt safe. Mom's disapproval and detachment had felt so much safer than friendship and caring about anyone when her father and friend could disappear seemingly of their own volition. Possibly even together.

She hadn't just been *left* to this life, she'd held on to this life because it was all she'd had.

She didn't want to anymore.

Which filled her with a sense of purpose. *Get your things.* She needed to get back to the Hart Ranch. Maybe they'd find some answers on what her father was involved in. Maybe they should. The guns, the warnings. He certainly wasn't involved in anything *good*, and he seemed to be… Well, he wasn't in control, was he? He'd said he couldn't stop them from coming after her if she kept poking.

Worry curled in her gut. She really wished Brody would stop digging, but he'd had a point. She'd always be looking over her shoulder if they didn't create some closure, and she knew from experience that was no way to live.

She blew out a breath as she considered the two entry points to the house. The side door would lead her to her room, and her side of the house where Mom almost never went.

But if she went in the main door, she could find her

mother and ask if Mom needed anything. She didn't *want* to do that, but guilt propelled her.

She didn't know why she felt guilty. Mom never seemed to feel anything. But there was some latent need in Kate to take care of her mother, even if Mom never returned the favor.

So she unlocked the front door, then frowned. She could hear voices from the room off the foyer. A man's and a woman's. Recollection and dread skittered down her back, but she had to be imagining things. She had to.

But when she stepped into the parlor, both her parents stood there. Arguing, clearly. For a moment Kate wondered if she'd stepped back in time.

But then she saw the guns in her father's hands.

BRODY WASN'T USED to impatience. It was something that had been drilled out of him in the military. Things took the time they took. A soldier needed to be patient. An elite soldier didn't let tension and adrenaline distract focus.

He didn't feel very elite, waiting for the sleepy county clerk to get his butt in gear and fulfill Brody's request. He felt like jumping over the counter and taking care of things himself.

But instead he sat in a hard plastic chair, in a small building that smelled of industrial cleaner, and waited. After eons the older man behind the counter shuffled back into view, holding a flimsy piece of paper. "Went ahead and copied it for you. It's owned by an LLC," the man finally said. "Stanley, Inc. LLC." He showed Brody the paper. Which told him nothing, but he supposed it gave Landon another avenue to investigate.

He slid the paper over the counter. "That'll be fifteen dollars."

A bit steep, and Brody hadn't *asked* for a copy, but he still counted out some cash and handed it over. "Thanks." He took the paper and stepped back out into the early afternoon sunshine. Blinding with all the snow on the ground, but not as frigid as it had been.

Brody walked back to his truck and got in. He called Landon and put him on speaker before pulling back out onto the highway.

"Owned by an LLC. No names of people, but the LLC name is just Stanley, Inc."

"Weird I couldn't find that online, but something to go on. Take me two minutes to figure out."

Brody drove as Landon typed away. "Owned by a Jonas Lantsey." More silence except for the clacking of computer keys. "Who's been dead for twenty years, so that doesn't wash. But I'll dig deeper on him. Might have something to go on once you get back."

"Kate back yet?"

"Don't think so."

Brody frowned. She'd been right. He couldn't keep her prisoner, and there'd been no specific threat against her. Brody did truly believe her father was keeping her safe. But he still didn't like the *potential* of mistakes. A man with a gun had shot at him. Someone in a truck had run them off the road.

Even if she wasn't a target per se, she wasn't *safe*. And he needed her safe.

"I'm on my way back. Call if you find anything truly interesting."

"Sure thing, boss."

Brody rolled his eyes at Landon's send off before he hit End on the phone. Then he typed in Kate's number.

If she wasn't headed back to the ranch by now, he'd just stop by the Phillips house and pick her up. Well, she had Zara's truck so maybe he wouldn't pick her up so much as follow her home. Keep an eye out.

It was better to be overcautious than careless. Something he had a feeling Kate needed to learn. Or maybe just accept his temporary protectiveness until they got to the bottom of everything.

He wasn't going to let something happen to her just because she didn't understand the full threat. He couldn't. And she had to know that, considering she'd been willing to give it all up to protect *him.*

Something that still leveled him, humbled him, made him feel awkward and far younger than a man who'd seen what he'd seen should feel. So he'd act. Rather than sit in all that feeling.

He hit Call on her number and waited while it rang. Her voice came over the speaker, encouraging him to leave a message.

She hadn't answered, which had a cold pit of dread forming in his stomach. But before he could truly panic, and start speeding toward Wilde, a text message from Kate dinged.

Just having lunch with Mom. Will call soon.

He supposed that was a good enough reason to not answer his call, but why was she having lunch with her mother who hadn't even known she was away from home the past few nights?

He chewed that over on the drive back home.

Chapter Seventeen

Kate was in a little bit of a daze. She'd been shocked to see her parents together, and then…she wasn't sure what had happened. Her head pounded and she opened her eyes, realizing she was in a sitting position.

Tied in a sitting position. To a chair. She'd passed out. No…no, something had happened. She willed her mind to part the fog that seemed to encompass it. She had been standing there, staring open-mouthed at her parents. Both of them. Calmly in the same room. Then Mom had stepped forward and…

Something had hit Kate in the head. Hard. Right where she was already hurt. Then everything had gone black.

She tried to reach her hand up to touch her head, but the lack of movement reminded her she was tied up. To a chair. She looked around the room. Still the parlor. Still her…parents.

Together. Standing in the same room, like ten years hadn't passed. Like Dad had never disappeared.

"You shouldn't have hit her so hard," Dad was saying to Mom.

Her mother had hit her? Her *mother.* And her father wasn't saying *you shouldn't have hit her* or expressing any sort of outrage. He was just scolding Mom about the *strength* of the blow.

"It got the job done, didn't it?" Mom replied.

"What's going on?" Kate rasped, surprised at how raw her throat felt.

They both turned their gazes to her. Mom looked furious. Dad looked…like he had back at the cabin. Angry, worried, frustrated. He was dressed in some bizarre tactical gear, guns strapped to him. Her father. The kind, warm music teacher.

But it was him. Somehow, it was him, and her mother had *hit* her, and she was tied to a chair.

"You came home at the wrong time. Figures. Making my life complicated like always."

It sounded like her mother. Like everything she would normally say. But Mom had hit her where she was already hurt and tied her to a chair. "I don't understand." *Any* of it.

Mom rolled her eyes. "No one asked you to, Katherine."

Kate closed her eyes. Everything swirled and nothing made sense. She wanted to just…sleep. Give in to whatever this was. Let whatever happened happen.

Her phone ringing jolted her painfully out of the daze she'd been falling into.

"Brody," Mom said, frowning at her phone. "Is that who she was with at the fort?" she demanded of Dad.

Dad shrugged. "Didn't get a name, but she doesn't talk to very many people."

They both looked at her again. "Well, who is he?"

Kate didn't even open her mouth. She'd give them nothing, because while none of this made sense, her mother had hit her. One of them had tied her to the chair. No one was trying to help her or save her. She was, essentially, their prisoner. Both of them.

Neither of them needed to know who Brody was. Ever.

Brody. He knew where she was. He would come looking for her when she didn't answer. Relief swamped her. She'd been afraid for him, but she knew he could take her parents. No matter what was going on, he could save her from this bizarre turn of events. Not just could, *would.*

"What's that smile for?" Mom demanded.

"I'm not smiling," Kate said, sounding like a guilty toddler even to her own ears.

"She never did learn to lie. A problem from the start," Mom muttered, still holding Kate's phone and pondering the screen. "He must know where she is and she's stupid enough to think he'll come for her."

"Must be the same guy then," Dad said, sounding tired. "Best to keep him away if we can. He's not your average loser."

Mom nodded. "We learned that lesson with the others, last month."

The others? What on earth?

Mom typed something into Kate's phone. Then she held it in front of Kate's face. "That'll buy us time, don't you think?"

Just having lunch with Mom. Call soon.

Kate was very afraid it would buy Mom the exact kind of time she was referring to. And nothing good would come out of that time. "Time for *what*?" she demanded. Nauseous. Her head hurt so much she wanted to cry.

Her mother had assaulted her.

"Don't worry about it," Mom said, with a smile. "You've wrecked my plans for the last time." She turned to Dad. "We have to kill her."

Kate knew she made some kind of noise, but her parents acted like they hadn't heard it. While they discussed *killing* her. Like they were discussing what to make for dinner.

"She doesn't know anything," Dad said, shifting on his feet uneasily. He rested his hand on one of the guns connected to his vest.

"She knows enough. She's got to be gone. Which actually solves this Brody person problem. We'll frame him for the murder. Should be simple enough. Then they're both out of the way."

"Marjorie, you cannot kill our own daughter."

"Of course not. Killing is *your* job."

Dad lifted his chin. "I won't."

Mom raised an eyebrow. "Interesting rebellion, Art."

"This is a line."

Mom shrugged. "Not my line. I suppose you'd rather ruin fifteen years of work? I suppose you'd rather die yourself?"

For the first time Dad looked over at her. There was conflict on his face, but that didn't warm Kate's heart any. The conflict wasn't over whether he'd save her or *not*. It was over whether he was going to kill her or…it seemed, let Mom do it.

Whoever he was now, these ten years later, however he'd maybe tried to protect her from afar these past ten years, he was *conflicted* about the *manner* of her *murder*.

He was not her hero. Beginning and end of story.

Kate wanted to cry, but knew she couldn't. She'd *finally* found a life in the aftermath of what had happened ten years ago, and she simply wouldn't give in. If she did, it wouldn't just be her life over. They'd frame Brody. Maybe he'd be able to prove he hadn't hurt her, but she wasn't about to be party to putting him through that.

She needed a plan. No matter how her head hurt. No matter how much it felt like she might throw up.

"She could join us," Dad said, but even Kate knew by the way he'd said it that it wasn't an option.

Mom laughed. Way too loudly and way too long. "*Join* us. That wasn't an option back then and it's hardly an option now. She's always been so depressingly strait-laced." Mom looked at Kate with a mix of scorn and disgust. "She *never* could have given us what we wanted."

"I'm not killing her, Marjorie. I've killed plenty, but I'm not killing my own daughter."

Mom raised an eyebrow at Dad. "You know what happens then."

"So be it."

Her father had…killed? The man who'd taught her to play the violin? Who'd put her up on a horse when she'd been a little girl at the county fair. Who'd driven her to school singing along with The Beatles?

I've killed plenty.

It was a nightmare. She was just having some very realistic dream. This was too much to take in.

Funny, how her mother's behavior wasn't all that shocking. Maybe *murder* was a little over the top, but Kate had never expected her mother to care about her. She'd made that mistake enough times as a child that even once Dad had left, she hadn't expected Mom's reassurance.

Mom picked up her own cell phone and held it to her ear. "We're going to need you," she said. "Art's refusing to do the job." There was a beat of silence. "Main house," she said, then pushed the phone back into her pocket. "Now, we wait."

Kate looked at both her parents. Wait. To die? No. She was going to find a way out of this.

She had to. For herself. For Brody. She *had* to.

BRODY RETURNED TO the Hart Ranch and frowned when Zara's truck was nowhere to be found. He'd hoped that Kate had returned it and Zara had taken it elsewhere, but a sinking suspicion in his gut made him very much doubt it.

He sat in the idling truck. He was low on gas, and he still needed to go check on the truck that had crashed and see when they could go about getting that towed and repaired. Having one truck between the six of them, with only Zara's truck and Hazeleigh's temperamental car as emergency backup wasn't going to work for long and Kate had said she was having lunch with her mother.

He should give her space.

Every instinct he'd ever honed in the military told him to ignore *space*, but he wasn't in the military anymore, was he? Even if Kate was in danger, it wasn't from terrorist groups bent on destroying entire cities and countries. It was from her father, who was maybe dealing with something shady. But small-town Wyoming shady.

He needed to ratchet down his theories. This wasn't the military. He forced himself to get out of the truck and walk inside. He'd check in with Landon on this Jonas Lantsey character, and then...

Then he'd check on Kate. If she didn't answer her phone, he was going over to the Phillips house. He didn't want to make her paranoid or fear every bump in the night.

But he had to keep her safe.

Zara and Hazeleigh were in the kitchen when he entered, and Brody realized that for all the issues the women had been through, they knew Kate. Who she was and how she acted.

"Would Kate ever have lunch with her mother?" he demanded. She wouldn't lie. Could it have been code? What kind of code was that?

Zara and Hazeleigh looked at each other, then back at him with surprise.

"She might," Zara offered. "Mrs. Phillips always had a way of making Kate feel guilty."

Brody wanted that to make him feel better, but all it

did was lower his opinion of Mrs. Phillips, which was already about as low as his opinion of his own mother.

But Hazeleigh was frowning deeper and deeper. "That was true when we were younger, but not really lately. I mean, Kate *would* have lunch with her mother out of guilt. But I don't know the last time Mrs. Phillips did anything *with* Kate. Usually she just orders her around and keeps her distance."

"She texted me that she was having lunch with her mother."

"I guess if she texted you, it must be true, but—"

Hazeleigh was interrupted by Brody's phone chirping. He took it out of his pocket. A text from Kate.

A few errands to run for Mom. I'll text you when I'm on my way back to the ranch.

She ran errands for her mother. He knew she did. He didn't want to feel paranoid, and what would following her around do? Make her fearful. She was keeping in contact with him, and she'd promised to call for help if she suspected anything.

"I guess I'm overreacting. She's going to run some errands for her mom."

"But you think something's wrong?" Zara pressed.

"I don't know." Which was a hard thing for him to admit. He could go into town, follow Kate around, make sure she was safe.

But he knew that wasn't what she wanted.

Landon walked into the kitchen. He nodded at the Hart women, then turned to Brody. "Got you a full mockup on this Jonas Lantsey. Not sure it'll help any though. He died long before Stanley Music was created—LLC or the fake piano company."

"Jonas Lantsey?" Hazeleigh asked.

"You know him?" Landon returned, surprised.

"I did. Sort of. He was Kate's grandfather. Mrs. Phillips's father. He died when we were kids. Right, Zara?"

Zara nodded. "Yeah. I remember that. Kate wasn't really close to him, but he was one of the richest guys in town. Owned the bank and a bunch of things. The funeral was a big deal for Wilde."

"I guess that lines up with what I found. I got a name on the wife, but didn't look too closely at the family. Just his business dealings."

"He's connected to Kate's parents. That seems..." Brody trailed off, thinking it through. Kate's father was the one who disappeared. He could have easily used his late father-in-law's name to start whatever shady dealings he was into.

The question remained why?

"I don't like this," Brody muttered. "This is far more complicated than some small-town crime."

"So was what Amberleigh was caught up in," Zara pointed out. "She disappeared the same day Mr. Phillips did."

"But the men involved in killing Amberleigh were arrested."

Landon tapped the counter thoughtfully. "Drug rings can have more than one branch, especially when you're dealing with low-population areas like this. They'd need to run to a bigger city to really make enough money to make it worthwhile. Let me pull on that thread."

Brody nodded and Landon left, likely headed back to his room and his laptop. He'd get to the bottom of it, and with that information Brody would be able to keep Kate safe. Permanently.

Zara was studying him and Hazeleigh was twisting her fingers together. Neither of them looked any more settled or comfortable than he did.

Zara looked at her sister, then back at him. "If you think something isn't right, maybe it isn't. Sometimes feelings are right." She gave Hazeleigh another enigmatic look.

"She told me she didn't want to feel paranoid again," Brody said. "I go around checking up on her every five seconds..."

Zara nodded and Hazeleigh studied him, which was odd. Usually she was a bit too skittish to look any of them in the eye. "Do you have anything of Kate's?" she asked. "Anything she touched recently?"

"Her bag is up in my room."

"Sometimes... Not always, but sometimes I can... I can just kind of feel if something bad is going to happen." She grimaced over at Zara. "I knew Zara was going to find something bad that day she found Amberleigh. It's the triplet thing, sort of, but sometimes it can be deeper. Kate could be... I just..."

Zara put her hand on Hazeleigh's shoulder. "Just get her something Kate might have touched today, and we'll see if Hazeleigh has a feeling."

"Don't get your hopes up," Hazeleigh said, making a

pained face. "I can't control it. It doesn't always mean things. I just..."

"I'll go get something," Brody said. He'd seen men with a sixth sense about things in the military. He'd never fully bought into it, but sometimes he'd seen a guy know something bad was coming. A gut feeling. An instinct. Brody didn't know what to call it, but at this point, he'd believe whatever might assure him Kate was safe.

Chapter Eighteen

Kate wasn't sure how much time had passed. She didn't allow herself to worry about it. She just focused on her restraints and thinking through all the different ways she could get out of them.

The ones around her hands were looser than the ones around her feet, which could work in her favor.

She hoped with everything she had inside of her that *anything* would work in her favor.

It would. It had to. Brody had said it himself. She was like those pioneers she loved to study and tell people about. She was resourceful and scrappy. She would hold on to their example.

Hopefully there were no more ugly surprises. She kept her gaze on her mother as she tried to loosen whatever had her hands tied behind her back and to the chair. It wasn't rope. It was some kind of bendable plastic. Like an old jump rope she would have had as a girl. It was thick enough that the knots weren't completely incapable of being untied.

Eventually.

Of course, even if she did untie her hands, she wouldn't

be able to untie her feet without arousing suspicion, and her father had guns. She did not.

Weirdly, neither did her mother. Who seemed…in charge of this whole incomprehensible thing. If her father really wanted to save her, he could simply turn those guns on her mother.

Which told Kate everything she needed to know about being saved.

She knew Mom had been texting Brody every once in a while with a new excuse why she wasn't home yet, but eventually… If she could stay alive until tonight, there was no doubt Brody would come for her.

There was something empowering about that. Knowing she had someone she could depend on. She didn't want him to risk himself for her, certainly didn't want him being framed for her murder any more than she wanted to die, so that only made her more determined to handle this herself. Or at least get accomplished what she could, and if he came in the end and saved her—well, it would be like they had done it together.

Doing whatever she could, however she could, would make him proud. It would make herself proud, and she wouldn't have to feel afraid anymore. If she managed to get out of this, she wouldn't be afraid of any damn thing.

She blew out a breath, the sick feeling in her stomach had ebbed a little bit, but the effort she was putting into untying the knots without drawing attention was making her hot. She felt flushed and unsteady. No doubt her mother—her *mother*—had given her another concussion. Kate didn't know much about that, but she knew it couldn't be good.

Of course neither was her mother wanting her dead.

Mom was sitting calmly on the antique couch Kate had never been allowed to sit on. Dad stood in the corner, arms crossed, looking angry but…resigned.

Every once in a while Mom studied her, then checked her watch. Kate had no idea what that was about, so she just stilled and waited for the moment to pass.

Then, once Mom's gaze went elsewhere, Kate got back to work on trying to undo the knots tying her hands behind her back. She was definitely getting somewhere, but she had to stop until she could figure out what to do with her untied hands.

Mom stood abruptly. "He's here."

Dad's hands dropped from their belligerent pose, and his expression blanked. Mom…fixed her hair, of all the incomprehensible things.

Kate could hear the loud halting steps of someone deep in the house.

After a few minutes of waiting, an elderly man stepped into the room. He was shorter than Mom, or maybe just a little stooped. He looked like he'd at one time been a little heavier-set and was still wearing clothes from that time. They hung off his almost sickly frame, and a big black cowboy hat swallowed what seemed like his entire head.

Kate could only see his chin and his gnarled hands. Not a young man, by any means. Not a strong man. He also didn't seem to have any guns on him.

Mom looked at him with a cool kind of…awe, or respect, or something very rare for Marjorie Phillips.

Dad looked at him with a wariness that did not help Kate's nerves.

"Do you know what a risk I've taken coming here?" the man rasped, taking off the overlarge black cowboy hat.

Kate gasped at the face revealed to her. She even shook her head. She couldn't believe it. This had to be... She couldn't even access what this had to be.

The man in front of her had died twenty years ago. He looked older now, but she'd never forget that imperious scowl her grandfather had *always* worn. It was on his face now as he took her in.

"Honestly, Marjorie, I told you years ago she wasn't suitable," he said, looking at Kate with unveiled distaste. "So *emotional*."

"She hasn't been any trouble. She's never been any trouble."

It was the strangest thing, her father standing up for her. Like he always had. She'd always cast him as the hero for that.

But he had guns. Mom and her supposedly *dead* father did not. Whatever he was, even standing up for her, Dad was not the hero.

"Honestly, him too," Jonas Lantsey said with the wave of a hand. A very-not-dead hand. Kate stared at it, mesmerized. She'd gone to his funeral. She'd watched her mother grieve...in her mother's way.

The entire town had come out for his funeral. There'd been talk of a statue.

Now he was here. Alive. Apparently part of this whole her-mother-wanted-to-kill-her thing.

"He's been a very effective enforcer otherwise." Mom sighed heavily. "I suppose it's understandable. He's a little too attached to the child."

Child. She was twenty-six years old. And *her* child.

"Should have had a boy," Jonas said.

"Well, clearly I've had a break with reality," Kate said. Out loud. Because honestly. This was…beyond insane. She'd been having trouble believing Brody—all perfect knight in shining armor—could be real, and interested in *her*, but he'd *felt* real enough. She'd accepted every moment up until this one, more or less.

But no. She'd actually died when she'd had that concussion. Or maybe earlier. Oh, she was in a coma. That would really make the past week make so much more sense. A very delusional coma.

"Would you shut up."

It was only her grandfather's sharp command that had her realizing she'd been speaking all those thoughts out loud.

Then she laughed. She couldn't help it. She was losing her mind. That only made her laugh harder, and harder, no matter how much everyone ordered her to stop laughing.

Then her grandfather—her *dead* grandfather whose funeral she'd gone to—stepped forward and backhanded her across the face.

Hard.

That stung. And grounded her in the fact that no matter how incomprehensible, this was reality.

She had to get out of here ASAP, because she was

going to wind up dead, no matter how closely she was related to all these people.

"I told you to shut up." He gripped her chin, surprisingly hard for his thin frame and the fact she knew he was eighty-three. "You are a pathetic little girl and no one is going to come for you. We'll make sure of it."

Kate smiled. It was reckless, but she couldn't help it. "We'll see about that."

He reared back again, a look on his face very familiar and she realized how many times when she'd been a child that he'd wanted to hit her. Just like this. But he hadn't.

She saw the way his gaze flicked to her bandage. He was going to hit her there again, just like Mom had. She'd lost consciousness, and she couldn't afford that again.

When his hand came down, she angled her head a little so he hit a slightly different spot. It still hurt. Desperately, enough to have her eyes stinging with tears and a gasp of pain to escape her mouth, but she allowed her eyes to close and her body to go limp.

Hopefully they thought he'd knocked her out. If they left her alone for even five minutes, she'd find a way to escape.

BRODY BROUGHT KATE'S backpack to Hazeleigh, not bothering to force himself to be calm. He hurried. He thrust the bag at Hazeleigh, and he waited impatiently while she took it and closed her eyes.

She frowned. She moved the bag from hand to hand, ran her fingers over seams. Her frown deepened and deepened, regret suffusing all her features. She looked at Zara first.

"It's okay, Haze," she murmured.

Sad eyes turned to Brody and she held the bag back to him. "I'm sorry. I really am. It's hard to force it. I thought maybe I could, but I don't feel anything one way or another."

Brody set the bag on one of the chairs and then thrust his hands in his pockets. "I'm sure it's fine. I'm sure." Of course the more he repeated *sure*, the less *sure* he felt or sounded.

"You know what? I'll text her that I need my truck back," Zara said, already pulling her phone out of her pocket. "Ranching emergency. If she doesn't say she's coming right home, we go get her."

Brody stood very still, fighting every last instinct inside of him. Because she'd asked him to give her space. Because she wanted to feel like her life was normal. He remembered the way she'd smiled last night, feeling like she'd found herself after a decade.

If he went barging in, he ruined that.

Unless she's in danger.

Zara hadn't waited for his approval. She sent the text with a flourish, and then they all stood there, still and waiting.

"She's typing," Zara said. Then frowned. "She stopped." Zara peered at her screen, and Brody had the sense they were all urging her to answer. Answer that she was on her back home.

Zara chewed on her lip, Hazeleigh twisted her fingers, and still no message came.

"Screw it," Brody muttered. "I'm going."

He swept out of the kitchen. He didn't have a clue what the Hart women's response was, because he was focused on only one thing.

Making sure Kate was okay.

He felt guilty, even now, getting into the truck. She wanted space, and freedom, and not to be thrust back into a bad mental place. He understood that, more than she probably thought he did. He knew how important finding a way to deal with the hard parts of life could be.

But he couldn't give her the space she needed now. Which was a terrible rock and a hard place, but he just… It wasn't who he was. To wait. To feel this uncertain, this torn.

If she hated him for it…

He paused for a moment, but only a moment. Because he'd take her hate over her blood on his hands. Someone had run them off the road, shot at him. Her father had warned her to back off and Brody hadn't. Maybe it wasn't the military, but it wasn't normal life either.

If someone had gone after her, it was his fault. He'd pushed, even after the warning. Landon was smart enough with computers to know how to cover his tracks, but maybe Brody's going to the county office had set off something.

Brody had to be *certain* he hadn't put her in danger. That was on him. His mindset. He'd deal with it, once he knew she was okay. He'd deal with anything if she was okay.

He was about to stomp the gas, but Cal appeared in front of the truck, looking disapproving and angry.

Brody clenched his teeth together and rolled down his window. He wouldn't have a fight with Cal. Not now.

"We need the truck," Cal said.

"Too damn bad." Brody jerked the truck into Drive. But Cal didn't get out of the way, and Brody couldn't back up because there was a tree behind him.

"I know you want to solve Kate's little mystery, but we have a ranch to run. You can't just—"

"Kate went to get some things from her house, and she hasn't come back yet. She won't answer my calls. I'm going to go make sure she hasn't been *killed*."

Cal studied him, eyebrows drawn together, lines digging around his mouth. Lines that hadn't been there a year ago. This year had put him through hell, and he still hadn't clawed his way out.

Brody wanted to soften, but he just kept picturing Kate back in the truck. Her head bleeding. Unconscious. He'd carried her through a blizzard, and she'd…

"Stay put. Three minutes," Cal said.

"Cal—"

"Okay, two. Do not go anywhere." Then he disappeared, reminding Brody of too many deserts to mention. He supposed that's what kept him sitting there in the idling truck. It wasn't so much just that muscle memory of Cal being the superior officer. It was… Cal.

Where he led, the rest of them followed. Fought. And won. They were a team. A unit. They had to move together, or they were just disparate parts, not sure where they belonged.

But there were no fights left. No missions. This was just life. At some point he'd have to stop overreacting.

But when Cal reappeared with Landon and Henry, Brody supposed he'd stop overreacting some other day.

Cal got in the passenger side, Henry and Landon squeezing into the back.

"You don't all have to come. She might not be in any trouble, really."

Landon shrugged. "And she might be. In which case, you'll need us. You're a *terrible* shot."

"I hope to God there's no shooting." Brody squeezed his hands on the steering wheel and tried to access who he'd been once upon a time. "I am *not* a terrible shot."

"Compared to Henry, you are."

"Compared to Henry, everyone is," Brody muttered, hitting the gas pedal.

Henry only tipped his cowboy hat he'd grown over-fond of in the months they'd been here. Because it hid his face, and discouraged conversation.

"This is probably overkill," Brody kept muttering. Trying to talk himself out of it. But he kept just driving toward the Phillips house. When she was probably in town. At the Mart. Or talking to her mother. Maybe she'd gone by the fort to pick up her things.

She was fine. He was an idiot.

"Your instincts are telling you it isn't overkill," Cal said firmly.

Brody might have thought it strange, Cal encouraging him to do something that wasn't laying low, but he understood things he thought Cal hadn't come to grips with yet. So he said it, gently as he could.

"We aren't in the military anymore, Cal. This is just normal life."

"Tell that to Jake who got shot trying to save this one just a few weeks ago," Landon said, jerking a thumnb at Cal.

"No one else is getting shot on my watch," Cal said grimly, squinting up at the Phillips house as it came into view. "Not us. Not anyone."

Brody concentrated on the snowy road, and it felt like a mission again. The four of them. Danger. Worry. But the cool determination to see things through without any loss of life.

They simply wouldn't allow it.

Chapter Nineteen

Kate listened, trying to file away all the information being passed from her mother to her father to her grandfather.

If she thought too deeply about it, she wanted to laugh again at the absurdity of it all. Or maybe cry. Either way, she had to keep her breathing even, her body limp and her eyes closed.

No matter how much her neck was starting to hurt.

They'd discussed *how* to kill her, which was surprisingly cold-blooded and easy. Shoot her in the head.

Kate could almost believe they were talking about someone else. In fact she tried to picture someone, *anyone* else.

But they were struggling to figure out how to coordinate framing Brody. That was buying Kate some time.

"You've been contacting him with her phone," Jonas was saying in his cold rasp. "We'll kill her in her bedroom, get him to come over."

"We could do murder-suicide," Mom suggested. "Cleaner."

"You'd have to time it right. The police can figure out

all those time-of-death things, and God knows people don't think you leave this house."

"I'll take a sleeping pill. If Art won't do the deed, you'll have to."

Jonas grunted, clearly irritated by that. "Might as well kill him too while we're at it."

"You're going to kill all these people over some money?" Dad asked.

"You've been killing people for over ten years for some money and power, Art. How is this different?" Mom demanded.

"She's our *daughter.*"

"You didn't care so much about our daughter's feelings when you were sleeping with her friend when they were teenagers."

Kate's fingers seemed to go numb and she tensed against her will. She waited for her father to refute those words. It had always been a rumor, one she'd even believed for a while, but when Amberleigh had shown up dead last month—with Dad having nothing to do with it—she'd believed it was a mistake.

A misunderstanding.

"Amberleigh has nothing to do with this," Dad said flatly.

"No, she doesn't. You're lucky you didn't have anything to do with her death. That would have been ugly. For you. We're not going down for any of this. I believe my father and I have always made that abundantly clear."

Kate wanted to throw up. Or maybe cry. Anything

but sit here with her head lolled to the side, her neck aching. Her whole body in pain. She wanted this over.

"We could let her go. You know, Kate. She's not going to tell anyone. She'll do what we say. She's always done what we say."

Mom scoffed. "You *are* delusional."

For once Kate agreed with her mother. Maybe she'd listened to her father, but she'd never been all that biddable. Maybe she'd *thought* of herself that way, because she could be guilted into things. But Brody had pointed out to her that she'd set up exactly the life she'd wanted in the ways she could.

She had to believe she could keep doing that. So she went back to work on the knots keeping her hands tied. She was so close, and she didn't want to listen to anymore of the callous way they talked about ending her life.

So she focused on her. On the knots. On some kind of freedom.

Kate managed to get a knot untied and nearly made a noise in delight and couldn't quite keep her body still. Not only did she move, but the plastic rope hitting against the chair made a noise.

Kate kept her eyes shut, lolled her head and moaned. She didn't blink her eyes open. She kept her breathing even. Everything depending on them thinking she was out of it. She moaned one more time, quieter this time, then stilled again.

And hoped with everything she was that they fell for it.

"Maybe you've killed her already," Mom said, sounding hopeful.

Kate had to keep her face utterly still, no matter how much she wanted to frown at that.

"She had that head wound before she came here. Then I hit it. Then you hit it. Perhaps she won't come back around."

"Perhaps," Jonas agreed, sounding unsure. "But we can't leave that to chance. Shooting is simpler, and easier to pin on someone. Particularly if we can kill him as well. I'll take care of Kate. You, Art, will take care of the man. Or we'll take care of you."

"Fine," Dad muttered.

Kate had to remind herself, over and over, not to react. Not to let that lance of hurt and all this confusion and *grossness* tense her features or make a sound. She had to make them think she was really, really out of it.

If they left her alone for even two minutes, she could get her feet free and then she could fight. She knew what she was against now. She wouldn't be taken by surprise. Unless her dead grandmother walked through the door, she supposed, except she half expected that now.

There was nothing left to surprise her. Her father had slept with a sixteen-year-old. He'd killed people. Mom wanted her dead. And her late grandfather was alive and pulling the strings. She still didn't know what they'd been up to for the past ten years, but she didn't care.

She just had to save herself. The police could handle the rest. She'd gladly leave it up to the police to handle the sickening rest.

"We'll need to get everything set up in her room,"

Jonas said. "Then get a message to the man. Get him here. Kill Kate. Kill him. It'll need to be close together but not too close together."

Kate wondered how she could come from all these people who were just coolly planning a murder like they were planning a family vacation.

"We'll map it out," Mom said. "Let's go see what kind of space we're dealing with in Kate's room."

She heard the sound of feet moving. Would they all leave? Would she really get her chance?

"You too, Art," Mom said sharply.

"What about Kate?"

"What about Kate?" Jonas replied. "Even if she wakes up, she isn't going anywhere."

Kate kept utterly still, but deep inside she was smiling.

That's what you think.

BRODY PARKED OUTSIDE behind Zara's truck. It was parked on the street rather than in the drive, but Brody didn't know if that was a sign or not that something was wrong.

"Maybe I should go up, knock on the door. By myself. See what's up."

Cal nodded. "What if something *is* up?"

"It's not like someone is going to shoot me on the doorstep. Be a little tricky to get away with that." But he looked up at the gloomy house with an uncomfortable chill running down his spine.

"Way to tempt fate," Landon drawled.

"All right, we all get out. But you guys stay behind.

Spread out, maybe?" Brody shook his head and let out a harsh laugh. "This is insane. We are back in the real world. I can't go treating my life like a military mission."

"Why not?" Cal returned. "Military missions and life have a lot in common."

Brody didn't have the time or the wherewithal for a debate on *that.* So he got out of the truck. If he was struggling to deal with reality, at least he wasn't alone. His brothers were here.

Henry studied Zara's truck, poked around the snow it was parked on. "If she ran errands, she's been back a while. Truck's cold and looks like it hasn't moved. So either she only parked once or she parked in a different spot the first time around."

Brody looked from Henry and Landon up to the house. It was dark. A little rundown. When he'd first come here to tell Kate he'd help her, he thought it looked like a haunted house from a movie.

His opinion on that hadn't changed any.

He couldn't say it felt like they were being watched, but there was something about the house. Deep, and dark, and secretive.

Appearances could be deceiving. This house could be as nonthreatening as any middle-class suburban neighborhood house.

But this was Wilde, Wyoming. And this was Kate, and it was the feeling deep inside that things weren't as they should be.

Brody looked at his phone, then went ahead and dialed Kate's number. Her last chance to assure him things were fine before he barged in. He swore. "Straight to voice mail."

"We'll fan out. See if there's anything to see."

Brody shook his head. "I'm just going to go up to the front door. Kate or her mother will answer and tell me I'm overreacting."

"We'll be flanking you, out of sight, to prove it," Landon said, clapping him on the shoulder. His cheerful, unbothered demeanor at odds with his words.

"Since when do you agree with Cal?"

Landon shrugged. "Since we found a dead girl on our property last month. Since Jake got shot. Since you got run off the road. Should I go on?"

Brody blew out a breath. "Fine. See what you can find. But it's going to be nothing." Nothing at all. He stomped toward the front door while his brothers melted away.

It didn't escape Brody's notice they were all armed.

There was going to be a reckoning coming for them all, when they stopped flinging themselves into dangerous situations and started accepting that ranch life in middle-of-nowhere Wyoming was their lot.

But for now he had to be certain there was no danger. Then deal with the embarrassing fallout when Kate answered and yelled at him for invading her space.

God, he hoped like hell he would end up embarrassed and yelled at and not just a few minutes too late.

The walk up to the door was long and winding. Strange the estate was so nice and so… He didn't want to say it was poorly taken care of. There was some visible effort—but like it was just too much space for whoever was expending the effort to truly accomplish anything.

He had a feeling he knew exactly who the person giving any effort was.

When he finally reached the front door, he hesitated. This was a new feeling. Hesitation. Uncertainty. It reminded him too much of being a child. Of wondering who would be home, or who wouldn't. Wondering what grandparent, or aunt, or uncle would take him in. Uncertain he'd ever have a chance to take the reins in his own life.

But he had, and maybe the military had been taken away from him, and maybe that had been his identity, but he didn't *need* it to be. He needed Brody Thompson to be his identity, and Brody Thompson needed to be a man of action.

His phone chirped before he could ring the doorbell. It wasn't a text from Kate like he'd hoped, but a text from Cal.

Two vehicles back here. A snowmobile and a Cadillac.

With the text was a picture, dim and hard to make out as it was clearly through some kind of garage window.

Brody frowned at the picture of the snowmobile. It was a common belonging in these parts, but he'd think if Kate had one, she would have suggested using it. From what he knew about her mother, he couldn't imagine she used one.

The Cadillac seemed even more out of place. Maybe it had been twenty years ago when the house had been nice, but it was a newer model—which meant it hadn't been sitting there like the house.

Brody looked up at the door.

Something was definitely not right here.

Suddenly all his uncertainty was gone. He was going to get to Kate right now.

But before he could act, the front door opened, just a hair, then stopped. Brody moved to the corner, out of sight, and listened.

Chapter Twenty

Kate waited, counting in her head. She had to at least get to five hundred before she dared move. Though she'd heard their footsteps leave, it was hard to differentiate three different people. Someone could have stayed behind.

She carefully opened one eye. The room seemed to be empty. She looked around. *Careful, careful.* She had to be both fast and careful.

When she was sure the room was empty, she got the ropes off her arms and reached down to untie the ones around her legs. Her fingers fumbled and her neck and head ached, her stomach heaved but she couldn't allow herself to throw up. That would be too loud. Even if all three people were in her room on the other side of the house. They'd know.

They'd come back.

Careful, hurry.

Once she had the ropes untied, relieved tears threatened. But she wasn't out of the woods yet. She jumped to her feet, then nearly tumbled over. A wave of dizziness coupled with legs that had fallen asleep. She managed to catch herself on the coffee table.

The slap of her hands onto the surface of the table was loud, but not echoing. Not as loud as falling would have been. She held herself there, willing her vision to stop wavering. Trying to get her breathing under control.

But she knew she didn't have this kind of time.

She pushed herself back upright, then closed her eyes. The world was spinning. Her legs were tingling, but at least that was feeling over numbness. She carefully took one step forward, still with her eyes closed, just testing, slowly, to make sure her legs would hold her up.

She blew out a breath and then opened her eyes. Her legs were holding her up. The world hadn't stopped spinning, but if she could reach out and hold onto things for balance, she could make it.

She reached for the chair she'd been tied to, then managed a few unsteady steps to the wall. She leaned against it, breathing too hard. A few tears had leaked out of her eyes, but nothing mattered except getting out of this house. To Zara's truck.

She couldn't call for help. Mom had taken her phone. But if she could get to the truck…

Kate managed to use the wall as support and get out of the parlor, but as she was telling herself she just had to make it to the truck, she realized she didn't have her purse. Which meant no truck keys.

"Damn it," she swore softly, then winced. No talking. No nothing. If she couldn't drive away, she'd just have to run. If she kept walking, maybe the dizziness would cease, and she could run.

She'd *crawl* if she had to. She would not stay here and let her family kill her.

She could see the front door now. She was almost there. Outside was freedom. Within her reach.

She heard nothing but her own heart beating hard against her chest. Her breath raggedly going in and out. Too loud. Her body was too loud, but she only had to get to that door.

She nearly cried out when her hand closed over the doorknob. She wanted to sob, and though tears began to fall in earnest, she blinked them away. She turned the knob, but before she could pull it open, she heard footsteps.

"Don't."

Kate slowly turned to face her father. He was at the other end of the wall. He had one gun in his hand.

Pointed at her.

Kate looked beyond him. No Mom. No Jonas. Just Dad.

"You have to let me go, Dad," she said, and though tears kept falling, her voice sounded strong. Commanding.

He took a few steps forward, and there was an uncertainty in him that gave her hope. Maybe he'd let her go. He didn't want to kill her. He was her only chance.

"You don't have to do anything, just turn back around and let me go."

But Dad shook his head, slowly moving closer and closer. "They'll kill me if I do."

"It sounds like maybe you deserve it." Maybe that wasn't the smartest thing to say, but honestly. He'd slept with a minor. He'd killed people. He was willing to let his own daughter die. He was not a good man.

"Don't make me do this, Kate. Come back in. Maybe I can talk them out of it, but I can't let you go."

"*Make* you do it?" There was a little pang inside of her, a desire to *want* to believe him, help him. Her father who she'd desperately missed and tried to find for ten years.

But he was lying. He had his finger around the trigger. He wasn't letting her go. He wasn't talking anyone out of anything. "I'm not making you do anything."

She wouldn't go back in there. She'd simply have to make a run for it. If he shot her...it was better than waiting for what they were planning. It would be harder to frame Brody if she tried to escape this house.

If she died, it would damn well be on her own terms. If she could get out of the door before he shot, maybe the door could… Well, she doubted it would block the bullet, but maybe slow it down enough that it didn't kill her.

Of course that would put a crimp in her escape plans, but again, it would make it harder for them to frame Brody. And there was always a chance she survived.

There was *always* a chance if she fought.

So she said no more, she jerked the door open and ran.

Or tried to.

BRODY COULDN'T HEAR what was being said, but he recognized the cadence of Kate's voice. He crept back out, carefully eased the door open another inch.

"Don't make me do this, Kate. Come back in. Maybe I can talk them out of it, but I can't let you go." It was a man's voice. A man who sounded at the end of his rope.

Never good, and certainly not the lunch with her mother or errands she'd been texting him about.

He sent a quick text to Cal to bring everyone around front. He wasn't sure what trouble there was, but it *was* trouble. And whoever was speaking was damn well not going to let Kate go.

But before Brody could act the door flew open, Kate barreling right into him and nearly knocking him over.

Because she was running. Instinct took over and he manage to grab her and pivot so they didn't fall, even as a gunshot exploded from within the house. Missing them both.

"Brody," Kate said on an exhale. She grabbed onto his arms, eyes wild and unfocused. "You're here."

"What's going on, Kate?"

"We have to run. They're going to kill me. We have to..." She tried to pull him away from the door, but she trailed off as Cal, Henry and Landon appeared.

"You brought everybody," she said, and she didn't sound mad. She sounded awed.

"Not everybody—"

"Down," Henry shouted, and out of pure instinct from having worked with his brothers for a very long time, Brody pulled Kate onto the cold snowy ground as gunshots went off.

Brody looked up in time to see a man step out of the house, but before the man could get a good shot off on any of the three men with guns, Henry shot the hand that was curled around his gun. On a wail of pain, and a spurt of blood, the gun clattered to the porch below.

Pushing Kate back and out of the way, Brody dove for the gun. He managed to get a grip on it, but the original owner kicked him hard in the stomach. The shot to the hand certainly hadn't taken him out because the blow knocked the wind out of Brody.

Still, he held onto the gun as the man reared back to kick him again, but Brody wasn't about to let that blow land. Brody managed to jump to his feet and deliver an elbow to the gut of the man. He swept the man's feet out from under him, and then nodded to Cal's approaching form. "Get that other gun off him. Got something to tie him up?"

"Yeah. Called the cops. They should be on the way."

Brody looked at Kate. She was too pale. Blood dripping from that wound on her head like she'd been hurt there again. She leaned up against the side of the house like it was the only thing keeping her up.

Before Brody could ask if she was okay, a shot sounded from somewhere else. Henry started shouting orders to Landon and they huddled behind the trucks in the street. Cal, Brody and Kate were protected by the overhang of the porch, but that meant Brody couldn't see where the shooter was, and he was too far away from Landon and Henry to communicate easily.

Brody heard sirens in the distance, but they were still far away. Another shot sounded from the shooter and the truck window exploded.

Kate let out a yelp of surprise. Brody went to her side.

"Oh my God. They're going to kill them. All of us."

Kate's knees buckled, but Brody held her up. Held her to him.

"No, they're not. How many?"

"What?"

"How many people are in the house?" Her eyes still looked dazed, but she furrowed her brow as if in thought. "Just two as far as I know. They… My whole family. I don't know what they were doing. Something bad. Mom and my grandfather…my *dead* grandfather. They wanted to kill me. Dad didn't want to, but he would have. He would have." Tears were streaming down her face, and she wasn't making any sense.

The cop cars were getting closer. They had gear. Tactical training. They were capable of handling this, Brody knew.

But he and Cal were more capable.

He looked over at Cal. He'd finished tying up the man who'd shot at Kate. Was that her father?

No time.

"We can take them out before the cops even get here," Cal said.

"Read my mind." He turned to Kate. "Kate. Look at me."

Her eyes didn't really focus, but she turned her head to him.

"Where are the people shooting?" he asked gently.

She blinked once. Twice. "I don't know unless I see what window they're shooting from." She blinked once, her eyes finally focusing. "Brody, you should let the police handle it." She looked past him to Cal. "The police can handle it."

Brody pressed a careful kiss to her cheek. "We can do it better, Kate. Promise." He pulled back. "Trust me, okay?"

She swallowed, then nodded. "I have to know what window. Let me—"

"You'll stay right here where you're safe." He pulled his phone out of his pocket, but before he could text Landon, the man Cal had tied up spoke.

"They're in the attic. Third floor, door at the end of the hall, stairs go up to the attic."

Brody looked at him and couldn't stop the sneer of disgust. He'd been ready to *kill* Kate. Brody wanted to crush him.

"Can we trust him?" Cal asked.

Brody looked back at Kate. She looked hurt, incomprehensibly destroyed, but only for a moment. Then she shored herself up. "Trust? No. But he wouldn't want them getting away and him taking all the blame."

"All right. You stay put, okay? Do not move from this spot. Landon or Henry will come move you when they can, or you can go with the cops if they get here. Do not come inside."

"I know the house."

"We can figure out how to get to the attic."

"It's a big house. Take me with you."

"You're hurt. You—"

Another gunshot went off, blasting out another window on Zara's truck.

"We don't have time to argue," Cal muttered.

"I'm only going to follow you," Kate said stubbornly, no trace of the confusion or tears from before.

Brody didn't like it, but they didn't have time. Every gunshot from above was doing damage to the truck Landon and Henry were hiding behind. There was nowhere else for them to go, and until Henry had the vantage point for a good shot, they were sitting ducks.

"Okay, let's go," Brody muttered.

"Wait. Give me his gun," Kate said, pointing to the man on the ground.

"Do you know how to use his gun?" Cal asked suspiciously.

"I'll figure it out."

Cal shrugged and handed it to her. Then they stepped into the house as a team.

Chapter Twenty-One

Everything felt surreal, but Kate followed Brody and Cal into the house she'd grown up in. A gun in her hand.

She wasn't as dizzy as she had been, and she had her feet under her now. Shock had been replaced by anger. By *fury.*

She'd been deemed unworthy by her family, disposable even. They had been callously ready to end her life.

Well, they were going to pay. In jail. Where they clearly belonged. All three of them.

Though Cal and Brody had led her inside, they didn't know where to go. Yes, they could have figured it out. She wasn't *necessary* to this mission, but she could help make it faster. Get Landon and Henry safe, and those local cops who might not be ready for a shooter from the attic.

She slid in front of Brody, keeping her footsteps light. She'd snuck around this house enough to know how to move through it silently. Like a ghost. She'd always been little more than a ghost here.

Now she understood why. Well, understood wasn't

the right word. She didn't *understand* any of this, but she at least knew what she had to do.

Up the first set of stairs, then the second. All the doors on the third floor were closed, except one in the middle. Which was unusual. As far as Kate knew, the third floor was usually locked up. Mom claimed she didn't use it, and Kate rarely came up here these days.

She turned to Brody and Cal and motioned them to come closer. "It's usually locked tight up here. That room is open."

Both men studied the open door, then nodded. Brody reached out and pulled her behind him. They were in charge now.

They crept forward, in a kind of crouch, both holding guns as if they were simply extensions of themselves. It was like watching a movie. Except she'd been intimate with one of the men doing all this.

She crept behind, trying to model the way they held their guns so she could be ready. So she wouldn't be a liability.

No, she refused to be that.

Cal swept into the room, Brody behind him. It was something like a dance. Since Kate didn't know the steps, she waited at the door.

They both crept around the room, utterly silent, looking in the closet and under things. Brody shook his head as he returned to the door.

Something creaked above them, followed by another gunshot. The shooter was definitely in the attic.

Brody and Cal moved forward again, toward the attic

door. It was closed, and Kate knew it would screech when they had to open it. But if the floor creaked above every time they got ready to fire their gun in the attic, then they only had to time it right.

She gestured Brody to move closer, and she whispered just that in his ear. He nodded. Then pulled his phone out and tapped a text to someone.

She assumed Landon and Henry outside. When she heard the faint echo of a gunshot outside, then the groan of the floor above, she understood.

He'd had Henry shoot at them even though he couldn't get a good shot. Then, when the gunshot rang out just above them, Cal jerked the door open.

"You stay here," Brody whispered in her ear. "Watch any entry point. Someone appears you don't recognize? Shoot."

Kate blinked. But then she nodded. Because she could do this. She *had* to do this. Not just for Brody, but for herself. To prove something… She wasn't what she'd imagined herself to be all those years of plodding along, alone, researching her father's disappearance in a sad bid to prove that it wasn't what it looked like.

No, she was strong. She'd built the life she wanted. She'd escaped, and now she was going to help bring her family down.

BRODY HAD BEEN in enough rickety buildings, particularly with Cal, to know how to navigate a loud staircase without letting anyone above know they were coming. It was about being light-footed, knowing where to step, and despite being a big man, knowing how to be graceful and agile.

He and Cal took their time. No matter what was going on outside, they could only focus on the inside. The here. The now. A silent surprise arrival.

Cal was in the lead because Brody had been talking to Kate, but as they reached the top of the stairs, they came shoulder to shoulder as best they could. To assess and enter the room at the same time.

They looked at each other, nodded, then stepped forward, guns at the ready. But Brody only saw one man. Crouched next to one window. The attic was full of bits and pieces so Cal peeled off to search, while Brody stayed on the shooter.

Who turned, eyes wide in surprise.

Which matched Brody's. The shooter was an elderly man. He barely looked like he could walk without assistance, even though he clearly held the gun that had been shooting at Henry and Landon.

It shocked Brody enough not to shoot. But the man's eyes went cold, and Brody knew a stone-cold killer when he came face-to-face with one. Which cut through the shock.

Brody shot. Though it was a strange feeling, he reminded himself that no matter how old the man was, and how difficult it might be for an elderly man to recover from a gunshot wound, he'd wanted to kill Kate. Her supposedly dead grandfather.

Cal moved forward after the man crumpled to the ground and took the gun. "Easy enough," he muttered.

There were groans coming from the writhing man, but Cal set the gun aside.

"On this score, but Kate's mother is in here somewhere. You take him down to the cops if they're here. I'll go find her."

KATE FOCUSED ON keeping her breathing even. Cal and Brody were taking care of the dangerous bit. She had led them where they needed to go, and now she was just sort of the lookout.

Nothing would happen. She wouldn't have to shoot. Everything would be fine.

For just a second she closed her eyes. Because even when this was all over, her life was irrevocably changed. *Fine* was going to be something she had to work hard for again.

When she opened her eyes, nothing had changed, but she still felt…on edge. Something in the air. Something around her. She felt…watched. She frowned, looking down the length of the hall. Nothing.

But the silence was oppressive, and her pulse skittered. She glanced back at the attic door. Cal and Brody had left it slightly ajar, but not enough that she could see their progress.

Kate blew out a breath. She was just getting paranoid. They were rounding up Mom and her grandfather and she was just the lookout. That was all.

A door at the opposite end of the hall creaked open. Kate readjusted the grip on her gun and pointed it in the direction of the room, heart suddenly galloping in her chest. But she would remain calm. Had to.

Maybe it was… Well, she didn't have a good answer for that. But she was the only one here. She had to deal with it. Carefully she moved closer to the cracked-open door, keeping her footsteps light, avoiding the places she knew would creak.

A head peeked out, just barely, just enough to see the perfectly coiffed brown hair Kate recognized as her mother.

"Stop," Kate ordered. Because *she* was in charge now. With a gun.

Mom's face slowly turned toward Kate. She sneered, then boldly stepped forward into the hall, as if the gun in Kate's hands didn't scare her at all.

"You won't shoot me."

Kate blinked in surprise. Her mother wasn't afraid. At all. Despite the fact Kate had a gun and she didn't appear to.

"You're a weakling and a coward. Put the gun down, Katherine. Before you hurt yourself." Mom just kept walking toward her and the thing her mother had never understood about her was that calling her names, telling her what she was or wasn't only made Kate more determined in exactly what she was. Who she was. Herself.

Kate did *not* do as she was told. But she nodded. "You're right," Kate agreed. "Not about the weakling and coward thing. The fact I'm standing here proves that you're wrong there, but you are right that I probably won't shoot. I'm not a good enough shot to know how to shoot you without killing you. And unlike you, I don't want to kill anyone. Actually, you don't want to kill anyone either. Dad and Grandpa had to do all the killing for you, didn't they?"

Mom's disdainful expression turned into a smile that had Kate's blood running cold.

"You know why?" Mom reached inside her jacket and pulled out a very small gun, pointing it in Kate's direction. The smile was terrifying without the gun, but now—Kate couldn't breathe.

"I enjoy it too much." Mom lifted her gun and Kate knew she had to save herself. She had to shoot first. But she *really* didn't want to kill anyone. Even the cold-blooded woman who'd birthed her and still wanted her dead.

A gunshot went off and out of pure instinct Kate flung herself onto the ground. But it wasn't her mother's shot. It was from upstairs.

Oh God.

Kate knew she didn't have time to panic about Brody and Cal. Mom was looking at the ceiling and this was Kate's only chance.

She regrouped, set herself up lying there on the ground and aimed as Mom's gaze came back down to her. As Mom's own grip on her gun tightened, aimed.

Kate didn't know who shot first.

A GUNSHOT FROM just below exploded before Cal had even carried the old man to the stairs.

"Kate." Brody jumped in front of Cal, practically scaled the entire staircase and burst out the door. Kate was sprawled on the ground, and he leaped forward and lifted her up with one hand. "Kate. Where are you hurt?"

"Brody." She let out a rush of breath. It might have been a laugh except nothing was funny. "I'm fine." She pushed at him, and he had to slowly get it through the haze in his brain that she was all right. He loosened his grip on her.

She looked down the hall. A woman was crumpled on the floor. Still.

Kate swallowed. "We shot at each other. She missed. I didn't." Kate was beginning to shake, so Brody slid his arm around her.

"Did I kill her?" she asked weakly.

"Here. Sit down." Brody helped her into a sitting position, then popped his head in to the attic stairwell. "We're good," he told Cal. "We'll get the cops and a paramedic."

Cal nodded. "I'll do a field dressing up here."

Brody turned his attention back to Kate. "You sit right here."

"Did I kill her?" she repeated, starting to go pale.

"Don't move."

Brody walked down the hall to the crumpled woman. He kicked the gun back toward Kate. A tiny thing that couldn't have done much damage from that distance. Kate's gun on the other hand had been of the high-powered sort.

Blood was beginning to seep out onto the floor. Brody couldn't tell where the woman had been shot, but he took a limp hand and tried to find a pulse. He breathed out a sigh of relief when he found one, though he wasn't sure how long that would last. "She's still got a pulse. We'll go on downstairs and find a cop. Get them up here. We'll need an ambulance."

Kate was by his side even though he'd told her to stay put. Still pale, still shaking, but very clear. "We can't leave her alone."

"Kate."

"Not because I care. Or maybe I still care, I don't know. The point is, she left me alone unconscious, and I managed to get away. Someone needs to watch her just in case."

"All right." He nodded. "I'll stay. You go get the cops."

She nodded. She looked at the puddle of blood slowly growing next to her mother. "I don't want to kill anybody, but if she dies… I know I had to do it."

"I know you did."

She nodded again, then turned for the stairs. By the time she reached the top, she was moving at a jog.

Brody blew out a breath and found himself in the very strange position of hoping a woman who'd tried to kill her own daughter survived.

For Kate's sake.

Chapter Twenty-Two

Everything became a bit of a blur after Kate ran downstairs. She found a cop. An ambulance showed up. Mom, Dad and her grandfather were taken away in one. Brody insisted on driving her to the hospital, though she felt fine. Maybe weak and a little dizzy, but she'd survived.

Turned out survival was a powerful healing force.

The hospital was even more of a blur, especially when they insisted Brody couldn't accompany her and she was on her own. Doctors and nurses poked, and prodded, and asked questions until everything around her felt like a buzzing cacophony of noise.

She'd passed out, which had earned her a CT scan and an overnight stay at the hospital. Once she was settled into a room, a parade of different kinds of police officers started to come in. She was asked questions, all sorts of nonsensical questions, over and over, by different officers. Some she recognized, some she didn't.

She knew she didn't have the answers they wanted. All she knew, even now, was that her family had been willing to kill her to hide whatever it was they'd been doing for the past ten years.

A nurse ushered in her next visitor, and though she was routinely disappointed it wasn't Brody, she managed to smile at someone she actually knew.

Thomas Hart was a deputy for Bent County, and cousin to the Harts. She'd grown up with him, and even though they weren't close, she knew he would give her some answers others wouldn't.

"How are you holding up, Kate?"

"I'm okay. What can you tell me?"

He itched a hand through his hair, looking a little sheepish. "It's a bit complicated as of yet."

"I know my family are bad people. You don't have to spare my feelings. They wanted me dead. Message received."

Thomas nodded, somewhat apologetically. "I can't tell you everything. Some federal agencies came in and they won't tell *me* everything. But Zara called me and asked me to give you a rundown on what I could."

Zara had called him. Zara cared. Maybe Kate had lost her family, but she'd gotten Brody and regained her best friend.

"It seems the Lantsey family, your grandfather and your mother in particular, have been creating a kind of drug-selling center. Multiple rings. Amberleigh was involved in one—the one we took down last month, but there were more. Your father was involved in almost all of them, and apparently his disappearance was tied to a tip coming through back then that he was involved in drugs. So he had to disappear or face an investigation from the feds."

Kate understood all the words, but it was still like it

was happening to someone else. About someone else. "My grandfather—who faked his death—and my mother and my father were all selling drugs."

"More or less. Running the organizations that sold drugs. They amassed quite a fortune doing it. We're working on search warrants that will help us bring down the remaining rings, but at the end of the day, you brought down a major drug operation, Kate."

"I didn't do much." Just shot her mother. She kept waiting to feel guilty about it, but too many mixed emotions prevented her from getting all the way there.

"All that information you collected for the past ten years? That's a whole heck of a lot. We've got years of stuff to go on, because of you. Which means the chances of them actually getting charged and convicted is higher. Be proud of yourself, Kate."

Proud. She didn't know how to be, but she appreciated Thomas coming on Zara's behalf. Now she had some answers. "Can I see Brody?"

"That's up to your doctor, but I'll see what I can do."

She managed a little smile, then settled back into the uncomfortable hospital bed. She wished she could… well, not go home, but go to her *new* home. She wanted to settle in Brody's bed at the Hart Ranch and bury her head in the sand for a few hundred years.

When the door opened next, exhaustion settled in her bones. But it was *finally* Brody. Who looked as exhausted as she felt.

Still, she asked him the one thing she hadn't been able to bear asking anyone else. "How's my mother?"

"She's alive still. From what information I could finagle, she made it out of surgery."

Kate nodded. "I don't want to ever have anything to do with her ever again, but I don't want to be the reason she's dead. I suppose that makes me weak."

Brody slid onto the bed next to her, wrapped his arms gently around her. "I think it makes you incredibly strong."

She smiled up at him. "Brody, you saved my life."

"*Helped* save your life. You did the vast majority of that."

She leaned against him and sighed. "You came. I was worried she'd convince you not to with all her texts."

"I talked myself out of coming a million times, so don't thank me too much."

She reached up, cupped his face. "But you came. No one else has ever showed up for me. Not like you have."

"I always will."

She didn't think it made any sense to believe him, but she did. So much. "Yeah, I think you will."

"You should probably stay at the ranch for a while, with me. Until things fully settle down. The feds will be crawling all over that house for a while."

She smiled to herself. "Are you asking me to move in with you?"

He stiffened a little, but it was kind of sweet. She'd seen him in action now, multiple times. He was this big strong military guy who knew how to carry her through blizzards and take down bad guys, but he still wasn't quite so sure about all this relationship stuff.

"I guess I am," he muttered. "Share a room, anyway. It comes with five annoying brothers, though."

"I always wanted siblings."

He kissed the top of her head. "You got them. And me."

"It's a pretty good deal," she said, snuggling in. No matter what happened with her family, she *had* gotten this pretty good deal. Through her own strength and determination, and a little help from a military man.

THE NEXT DAY, Brody was allowed to bring Kate home to the Hart Ranch, what was becoming the Thompson Ranch, he supposed. She was definitely a little worse for wear, but the doctor had been pretty positive about the prognosis. She might suffer from headaches for a while, but as long as no further brain injuries happened, there shouldn't be any lasting effects.

Brody was determined to make sure of it.

She was quiet on the drive home, and he didn't press. She had a lot to work through. A lot to deal with. It didn't surprise him she was handling this better than he might have imagined. He'd stopped being surprised by her strength and simply learned to be in awe of it.

Brody parked and helped her out of the truck. She leaned her head on his shoulder as they walked up the shoveled path. "I always loved this house."

"Well, it's yours as long as you'd like."

They stepped inside and everyone was there. There was a big banner on the wall that that said Welcome Home, Kate, and streamers.

Kate laughed. "You guys. This is too much." She looked up at him, but he shook his head.

"Don't look at me. I had nothing to do with it."

Her gaze roamed over the small crowd in front of them and then she moved forward and wrapped Zara and Hazeleigh in a tight hug. Zara looked uncomfortable, but she patted Kate's back awkwardly while Hazeleigh sniffed and murmured a few things Brody couldn't hear.

"Stay as long as you'd like, Kate," Cal said, as if he spoke for all of them. "Especially if you keep cooking for us on Brody's turn."

"Here, here," Landon readily agreed.

"Thank you. Really. All of you. For…everything. Cal. Henry, and Landon, and… You put yourself in some danger for me, and I…"

"It's nothing," Henry said gruffly.

"Part in parcel when falling in with the Thompson brothers," Landon drawled with a wink.

"All right, I'm going to have to break this up. Doctor's orders. She's got more resting to do," Brody interrupted.

"Good, you lazy lot are behind on ranch chores," Zara said good-naturedly, as she began to shoo them in different directions.

Brody helped Kate upstairs. She was definitely dragging.

"I don't know how," she said through a yawn as he followed her into his room, "but I am tired."

"You've been through a lot. I can't imagine you slept well last night in the noisy hospital. You should sleep now and get all caught up." He nudged her into the bed, pulled the covers up over her. She smiled sleepily up at him, patting the small sliver of bed next to her.

"I know you've probably got a million things to do but stay for a few minutes."

Minutes seemed so paltry, and she seemed so...perfect. Just lying there, smiling up at him. How she'd come through all this, he didn't know. He only knew that the powerful feeling that swept through him wasn't going away.

"I love you, Kate."

Her eyes had been drooping sleepily, but now they popped wide open, something like shock slackening her features. "Oh," she breathed. "Are you sure?"

He wouldn't have thought anything she could say would have made him laugh. Not when every muscle in his body felt like it had turned to heavy metal. Not when for so long he believed love couldn't be real.

But he loved his brothers. And he loved Kate. He was exceptional at many things, so he'd figure out a way to be exceptional at loving her. No matter how it scared the hell out of him.

He took that seat next to her on the bed. "There isn't a thing I don't like about you. You're smart and funny. Every time I think I've got you pegged, you turn out to be something else. You've got all those shy trappings, but at the end of the day you're so determined you never let your fear stop you. You've been dealt all these blows, and you keep fighting. Trying to make a place for yourself. You stopped depending on anyone else to make it for you and I don't know, I guess that makes me want be the one you depend on. So, yeah, I'm sure."

She pushed up into a sitting position and flung her arms around him. "I love you too. No one's ever seen me the way you do, and you make me see myself the way I am. I don't know how I could have done all this without you."

He held her tight. Kissed her cheek. He felt a little off-balance. For a lot of reasons, but...she was right.

She pulled back, tears in her eyes but they didn't fall. "I know it'll take a while to really process what they did, what losing them means, but I have you. And Zara and Hazeleigh. And brothers, I think. So, it'll all be good. No more lying, and secrets, and all that. Just... normal life."

Secrets. Brody practically winced. He had some of those. Ones he wasn't supposed to tell.

But how could he keep them from her after *that*?

"There's something I have to tell you."

Her face didn't fall exactly, but a wariness crept in. "Oh."

He took her hands in his, tried to find the right words. The right balance. He couldn't tell her everything. It would be a dereliction of duty—not to the military, but to his brothers.

"Kate... There are things I can never tell you."

She tugged at her hands, but he held firm, looking up at her. Maybe a little desperately. "Hear me out. Give me a chance.... They're military things. Reasons we ended up here..." He shook his head and knew he was already botching it. "We were a military group. All of us who moved here. From different branches and backgrounds, recruited to do dangerous missions because... Mostly because we were elite soldiers who didn't have any family to hold us back."

Kate chewed on her bottom lip, but she stopped trying to withdraw her hands.

"Our job was to find, research and ultimately stop and take down terrorist organizations. We did that for years, and successfully. Our team got quite a reputation, which meant that we were targets. There was an intelligence breach and our identities were found out. Long story short, the military killed us, on paper, and gave us this new life."

Her eyebrows were furrowed, and she was clearly considering his words.

"So, your name isn't Brody?"

He managed a small smile. "Adam Brody Calhoun. I always went by Brody though. But I'm not him anymore. He's dead. That probably doesn't make sense to you, but it's the only way..." Brody shook his head. "I'm sorry, Kate. I should have told you sooner. Or..."

Kate touched his cheek. "I'm glad you told me so I can understand." She smiled at him when he finally looked at her. "That's the kind of secret that doesn't matter all that much because that was your past. I'm glad I know it, but you're right. I don't need the details unless you want to give them. I just need you. Here. This is your future."

He looked at her for the longest time, half convinced she couldn't possibly be real. But she was here. And his. "I never really thought about my future, but this is more than I could have dreamed."

"I think we both deserve a little more than we could have dreamed."

Yes, they did—and they'd have just that.

* * * * *

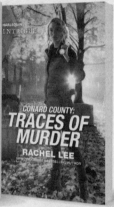

COMING NEXT MONTH FROM

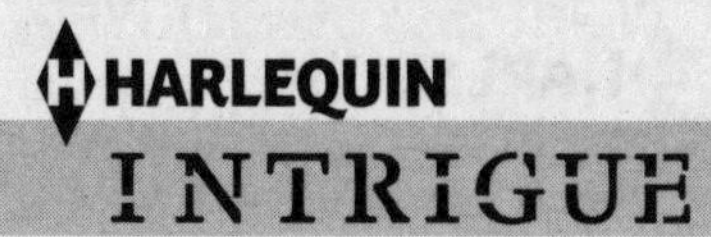

#2109 CHRISTMAS RANSOM

A Colt Brothers Investigation • by B.J. Daniels

Former rodeo star Davy Colt traded his competition spurs for a PI license. But even after years away, he never stopped loving hometown sweetheart Carla Richmond. When a robbery and hostage situation at the Lonesome bank leaves the loan officer injured and shattered, Davy will ransom his heart to avert a deadly Christmas for Carla.

#2110 CANYON KIDNAPPING

Eagle Mountain Search and Rescue • by Cindi Myers

Haunted by tragedy, Search and Rescue volunteer Sheri Stevens is determined to help find a missing child. Erik Lester, lead detective—and Sheri's ex-husband—is also dedicated to bringing the little girl home. As reigniting passion forges an even deeper bond between them, is this their second chance to vanquish the ghosts of the past?

#2111 DECODING THE TRUTH

Kansas City Crime Lab • by Julie Miller

A vicious hacker has KCPD lab tech Chelsea O'Brien dead in his sights, and Robert "Buck" Buckner won't let his personal heartbreak prevent him from keeping her safe. But the sparks between this reserved ex-cop and the warmhearted Chelsea are as hot as the trail they're tracking.

#2112 LOST IN LITTLE HAVANA

South Beach Security • by Caridad Piñeiro

Detective Roni Lopez has been keeping a secret from Detective Trey Gonzalez her whole life. When his partner is gunned down, she has a new secret to keep. But with their lives on the line, she has to make some tough choices about what really matters...

#2113 WYOMING CHRISTMAS STALKER

Cowboy State Lawmen • by Juno Rushdan

After Grace Clark witnesses a brutal murder, she tumbles headlong into a world of motorcycle gangs, cults and a young girl's secrets. Chief deputy sheriff Holden Powell's determined to discover what's wreaking havoc on their town this Christmas. He has something to prove, and he won't let anything happen to Grace—not on his watch.

#2114 BACKCOUNTRY COVER-UP

by Denise N. Wheatley

When her body is found on a hiking trail, deputy sheriff Todd Jacobson believes his sister was murdered. Her best friend, private investigator Elle Scott, agrees to help Todd prove it. Before long, Todd realizes he's Elle's only hope against becoming a corpse under the tree this Christmas.

Read on for a sneak peek at
Christmas Ransom,
the third book in New York Times *bestselling author*
B.J. Daniels's A Colt Brothers Investigation series.

The whole desperate plan began simply as a last-ditch attempt to save his life. He never intended for anyone to get hurt. That day, not long after Thanksgiving, he walked into the bank full of hope. It was the first time he'd ever asked for a loan. It was also the first time he'd ever seen executive loan officer Carla Richmond.

When he tapped at her open doorway, she looked up from that big desk of hers. He thought she was too young and pretty with her big blue eyes and all that curly chestnut-brown hair to make the decision as to whether he lived or died.

She had a great smile as she got to her feet to offer him a seat.

He felt so out of place in her plush office that he stood in the doorway nervously kneading the brim of his worn baseball cap for a moment before stepping in. As he did, her blue-eyed gaze took in his ill-fitting clothing hanging on his rangy body, his bad haircut, his large, weathered hands.

He told himself that she'd already made up her mind before he even sat down. She didn't give men like him a second look—let alone money. Like his father always said, bankers never gave dough to poor people who actually needed it. They just helped their rich friends.

Right away Carla Richmond made him feel small with her questions about his employment record, what he had for collateral, why he needed the money and how he planned to repay it. He'd recently lost one crappy job and was in the process of starting another temporary one, and all he had to show for the years he'd worked hard labor since high school was an old pickup and a pile of bills.

He took the forms she handed him and thanked her, knowing he wasn't going to bother filling them in. On the way out of her office, he balled them up and dropped them in the trash. All the way to his pickup, he mentally kicked himself for being such a fool. What had he expected?

HIEXP0922

No one was going to give him money, even to save his life—especially some woman in a suit behind a big desk in an air-conditioned office. It didn't matter that she didn't have a clue how desperate he really was. All she'd seen when she'd looked at him was a loser. To think that he'd bought a new pair of jeans with the last of his cash and borrowed a too-large button-up shirt from a former coworker for this meeting.

After climbing into his truck, he sat for a moment, too scared and sick at heart to start the engine. The worst part was the thought of going home and telling Jesse. The way his luck was going, she would walk out on him. Not that he could blame her, since his gambling had gotten them into this mess.

He thought about blowing off work, since his new job was only temporary anyway, and going straight to the bar. Then he reminded himself that he'd spent the last of his money on the jeans. He couldn't even afford a beer. His own fault, he reminded himself. He'd only made things worse when he'd gone to a loan shark for cash and then stupidly gambled the money, thinking he could make back what he owed and then some when he won. He'd been so sure his luck had changed for the better when he'd met Jesse.

Last time the two thugs had come to collect the interest on the loan, they'd left him bleeding in the dirt outside his rented house. They would be back any day.

With a curse, he started the pickup. A cloud of exhaust blew out the back as he headed home to face Jesse with the bad news. Asking for a loan had been a long shot, but still he couldn't help thinking about the disappointment he'd see in her eyes when he told her. They'd planned to go out tonight for an expensive dinner with the loan money to celebrate.

As he drove home, his humiliation began to fester like a sore that just wouldn't heal. Had he known even then how this was going to end? Or was he still telling himself he was just a nice guy who'd made some mistakes, had some bad luck and gotten involved with the wrong people?

HIEXP0922